GLYNDŴR

TO·ARMS!

I Delyth

Er cof annwyl am
Moelwyn Jones (1943–2015)

GLYNDŴR

TO·ARMS!

MOELWYN JONES

With grateful thanks to my family:
Dylan, Bethan, Ffion, Gwennan and Catrin,
and also to my wonderful friend, Iris Cobbe,
for all their support.

Delyth Jones

First impression: 2017
© Moelwyn Jones family & Y Lolfa Cyf., 2017

Cover illustration: Teresa Jenellen

ISBN: 978 1 78461 403 4

Published and printed in Wales
on paper from well-maintained forests by
Y Lolfa Cyf., Talybont, Ceredigion SY24 5HE
e-mail ylolfa@ylolfa.com
website www.ylolfa.com
tel 01970 832 304
fax 832 782

1

AFTER SEVERAL HECTIC and violent years, Christmas 1403 at Owain's temporary winter quarters in the heart of Snowdonia has given me a haven of quiet contemplation, following all the sadness of losing friends and loved ones in war. The remembered, nightmarish screams of the horribly maimed or dying in battle have faded a little in this cold, beautiful mountain retreat. The remote silence of this place has gradually saturated my soul with a soothing balm. It has also allowed me to put this terrible period and, indeed, my whole life into some kind of perspective. I still have an unsettling sense of foreboding when I think of more conflict to come. It is something I have never experienced before. Perhaps I am getting old… but enough of these foolish thoughts. I have a story to tell…

I was born in the beautiful Clwydian hills on a smallholding where my parents, in common with many other small farmers, struggled to eke out an existence keeping sheep and a few cattle. We also grew root crops for family consumption and, if there was any produce to spare, for sale in the local market. I was the youngest of four boys and the only one cursed with my affliction. Like my three older brothers, I grew up to be big and strong. In fact, when I reached the age of sixteen I was the biggest. Unfortunately, I was different in that I was totally hairless. Not a single hair ever grew on my body. I was bereft even of eyebrows and eyelashes. Nobody in the area had ever seen a specimen like me and in many ways I found myself ostracised. I was never truly accepted as a normal member of the family even by my brothers and my father. Many others in the neighbourhood made no effort to hide their view that I was a freak of nature, to be avoided if at all possible. The only one who treated me as a normal human being was my dear mother, who loved me more than any other, to the jealous annoyance of my brothers and even my father.

Fortunately, I was fond of studying and my parents soon realised that I had a gift for creating poetry. Later, I developed a fine baritone voice with which to sing my poems in the fashion of the day. We belonged to an impoverished branch of a family of *uchelwyr* and my kinsman Iolo Goch (Iolo the Red – on account of his long, flaming locks) was the leading Welsh poet of that era, unsurpassed in the use of the poetic form called cywydd. My father sent word to Iolo that he had a son showing much poetic promise, and asking him whether I could be sent to his home in Coed y Pantwn at Llechryd, near Denbigh for proper training as a bard. A few months before my sixteenth birthday I received a message from Iolo Goch inviting me to Coed y Pantwn to spend time with him to 'explore the magical world of poetry' as he put it.

I was not at all sure that I wanted to do this. Yes, it would be a privilege to study with the renowned Iolo Goch and he would also teach me to play the harp; every self-respecting bard provided his own accompaniment on the harp. He was known as a man with a very sharp mind and a wide store of knowledge encompassing many subjects, including the turbulent history of the Welsh, the legends of Merlin and the fabled stories of the Mabinogion and the Gododdin. He would be a wonderful teacher.

On the other hand, he was very eccentric. He dressed in what he described as the black robes of a druid, embellished with symbols and diagrams of the sun, the moon and the stars as well as other strange signs, the meanings of which were known only to devotees of the druidic religion. A self-confessed heathen, he flatly rejected Christianity and would not attend a service, or any other occasion, held within a Christian church. For a man who could conjure up such beauty and refinement in his poetry, Iolo could be exceptionally loutish and crude, in word and deed. There were times when he seemed to take delight in shocking people. Yet, when he sang wonderful poetry in his honeyed tenor voice, the very same people who had previously been shocked would find themselves spellbound and ready to forgive his earlier crassness. When in a good mood, he could be extremely humorous, and though he never married, his reputation as a lover was legendary.

It was clear that, with the exception of my mother, everyone else was eager to see me leaving for Coed y Pantwn, which was a day's journey on foot from our home. It would mean one fewer to feed, of course. After some thought, it occurred to me that if I did become a bard I could lead a comfortable life, mixing with influential people and being given free bed and board in the homes of many of the *uchelwyr* or squirearchy, in return for providing entertainment of an evening with harp and voice.

When, at last, I arrived at Coed y Pantwn in the little hamlet of Llechryd I stopped outside the gate, overawed by the stone-walled cottage which seemed a great deal bigger and grander than our little timber-built dwelling. As I knocked on the heavy, arched oak door I shifted uncomfortably from one foot to another. It was several years since I had seen my kinsman. Would he even recognise me?

'Upon my word, it must be young Gruffudd, Meg's son,' Iolo exclaimed as he peered up at me in the fading light. 'My dear boy, you have become a man... and a mighty one at that! By the power of sweet mistletoe, you are truly the biggest man I have ever seen. No wonder they call you Gruffudd Fychan! Why, you must be six feet seven inches tall, if not more. Well, don't just stand there, come in, come in. You must be tired and hungry, for you have travelled far.'

Iolo turned and led the way along a flagstoned corridor and through another doorway into a square room, comfortably furnished with a large fireplace and a banked-up log fire. Its long tongued flames lapped at the base of a large iron cooking pot, which steamed and bubbled merrily, sending a delicious aroma of lamb stew to assail my nostrils.

Soon we were both seated at Iolo's table devouring large bowls of hot lamb stew laced with root vegetables, and drinking ale from tall pewter tankards. After the meal, feeling comfortably full, we sat facing each other on the wooden settles either side of the fire. There was much to talk about and plenty of good ale to drink. Hours later, we climbed a creaky staircase and retired to our respective bed chambers. I felt happier than I could remember, full of good food and ale and secure in the knowledge that Iolo was a man I could get on with, and whose welcome to Coed y Pantwn was a warm and sincere one.

We breakfasted the next morning on bread and cheese washed down with small beer. Wasting no time, I was given the task of cleaning out the fireplace and preparing the evening's fire, refilling the cleaned grate with dried logs from a large cauldron set close to the hearth. Meanwhile, Iolo was busy in an outbuilding cutting up more logs with an axe before bringing them indoors to finish drying out.

Later, I had my first poetry composition lesson. First, Iolo spent some time assessing my knowledge of famous Welsh bards and poems, including the greatest poet of them all, the late Dafydd ap Gwilym, who had died of the Black Death as recently as 1350, and who was already being lauded as a poet of European significance. With characteristic lack of modesty, Iolo waxed eloquent about the best known of his own cywyddau. He then moved on to my taste in poetry and to examine some of my own crude attempts at composition. In truth, it was a morning which we both thoroughly enjoyed, and which I found both fascinating and instructive.

While continuing the poetry lessons Iolo decided, a few days later, to introduce me to the instrument so essential to all Welsh bards – the harp. He possessed a beautiful harp which he used whenever he performed in public. He also owned an older, much used harp which was still perfectly functional, being whole and easy to tune, but with its once smart wooden frame grossly disfigured by years of rough usage. It was the perfect instrument on which to learn the basics, my kinsman assured me. Unlike the poetry, learning to play the harp proved a real challenge for both pupil and teacher. It also revealed that the tales about Iolo's temper matching the colour of his hair were correct. My problem was a physical rather than a musical one. While he quickly established that my musicality, sense of tone and timing were fine, he came up against an obstacle which he had never before faced as a harp teacher. It was, in a word, hands – my

9

large hands, and particularly fingers, and their relationship with the closely-set harp strings. I was a quick learner and could soon pick up all the correct notes in a given melody. Unfortunately, I could not play them without adding other, extraneous notes, never intended by the composer, which changed the whole complexion of the melody and, alas, Iolo's temper.

One afternoon, Iolo snapped. He had spent nigh on two hours trying to get me to play a simple melody without adding extraneous notes, with little success. Suddenly, his face went red. He jumped to his feet and roared 'No, no, no... you stupid oaf,' and as I rose also, not knowing where this was leading, his arm swept over in an attempted slap across my face. I quickly raised my own arm and caught his wrist, stopping his arm halfway through its intended arc. For a moment we stared at each other, our faces very close. He had a murderous look in his eyes.

'No,' I hissed. 'I made a vow on my fourteenth birthday that I would never be bullied by anyone. Do not attempt to strike me again.' I let go of his wrist and the madness slowly faded from his eyes.

'Why I... I don't know what came over me. I'm... I'm sorry lad...' And looking a little shamefaced, he walked slowly out of the room.

Neither of us ever mentioned the incident after that, but it was never repeated. Amazingly, the very next day I finally conquered my problem with the harp. I was getting some practice in when Iolo entered the room. It was only when he stopped in his tracks and started laughing and clapping his hands that I realised I had just played the previous day's melody right through, without a single false note. Two months, and a lot of hard work later, Iolo pronounced himself satisfied that I had learned enough of the art of poetry and established a workmanlike command of the harp.

'Gruffudd, my boy, it is high time we took to the road so that you can begin your career as a working bard.'

It was the custom for bards to find favour with one or several of the *uchelwyr*, and to be invited for varying amounts of time into their households to entertain the family and their guests. His foremost patron at the time was one Ithel ap Robert, an Archdeacon of St Asaph Cathedral, who lived near Caerwys. He decided to inform the archdeacon that he was coming on one of his regular visits, and bringing with him a new young bard of considerable promise.

'But what will he say when we arrive and he sees me, another mouth to feed, when he has never heard of me?'

Iolo drew himself up to his full height. 'My dear young man, you forget that I am the leading poet of the day. Believe me, if I say I bring a bard of promise with me it will be accepted without question. Do you also forget that I am the son of Ithel Goch ap Cynwrig ap Iorwerth Ddu ap Cynwrig Ddewis Herod ap Cywryd, of Lleweni Manor in the Vale of Clwyd? Do you not realise that my lineage makes me an *uchelwr* too?'

I grinned. 'With a name like that who could possibly argue the point.'

He smiled broadly. 'It's that kind of incisive comment which proves you are my kinsman, Gruffudd.'

That first evening at the palatial home of Archdeacon ap Robert is firmly seared in my mind. It was my first outing as an accredited bard. I found myself called upon to provide a musical item following similar offerings from two other little known bards, before the great master, Iolo Goch, would be called upon to provide the highlights of the evening, a little later. This baptism into the bardic world, however, is not why the evening is etched so deeply into my memory. No, that takes second place to my first sight of the lady who was to light up my life. Alas, the initial joy of seeing her would soon turn into a heart-rending mixture of yearning and admiration for the only lady I would ever truly love, yet barred forever from telling her, or anyone else, of my feelings for her. The availability or otherwise of the object of one's love is immaterial; the heart only ever speaks once. It was a love fated not to be, for she was already spoken for.

When I rose to sing my evening's poetic offering, however, I had no way of knowing that she was beyond my reach. By chance, I had chosen a poem of mine which was a reworking of an old folk tale about a young couple who had fallen in love, only for the girl's father to forbid the union, believing that the lad was not good enough for his daughter. One evening there was a furious row between father and daughter and, in a rage, the father threw her out of the house into the darkness and the rain. Beside herself with sorrow for her lost love and convinced that she was bereft of any hope or future, she threw herself into the swollen river nearby. Her dead body was discovered in the cold waters some miles downstream the next morning. The words were shamelessly melodramatic, the melody slow and haunting, and my rich baritone at its most mellifluous, each note ringing clearly and crisply in every corner of the great hall, while my fingers danced over the strings of the battered old harp, plucking every nuance of emotion from each one. Though I say it myself, the item was a sensation and the ap Robert family and their guests were delighted with me. The applause lasted for several minutes and I was not allowed to take my seat until I had performed another poem. The lady who had so unknowingly galvanised me, and her father, were among the most appreciative in the audience and I was gratified to see that the lady kept dabbing a tiny lace kerchief to her eyes repeatedly, a response shown too by many of the other ladies present. When I finally resumed my seat I stole a glance at my kinsman who was staring disbelievingly at me. A plethora of emotions chased each other across his face ranging from shock to naked jealousy, but all overridden, eventually, by a warm smile of pride.

When we finally climbed an elegant spiral staircase to our sleeping quarters, Iolo belched heartily and said, 'What a wonderful meal that was, eh Gruffudd? And as for you my boy, don't you dare upstage your old teacher ever again.' He turned to me with a broad grin as he said this before adding, 'I have heard you sing that tale before but never as you did it tonight. What is more, your harp accompaniment was exceptional, and worthy of a far more accomplished harpist. You were truly inspired.'

Coming from Iolo Goch, that was praise indeed.

'Why thank you, Uncle, I never thought I would hear such praise from your lips.'

'Believe me, that kind of praise is not given lightly. You concentrated my mind for I knew that after your performance I was going to have to work hard to maintain my own reputation.' He laughed again as he reached the door of his bed chamber. 'Before coming here you were concerned that nobody would have heard of you. Well, after tonight, your fame will spread and everybody who is anybody in north Wales will be inviting us to visit – but to hear you, not me,' he chortled again before adding, 'Did you notice a well-dressed, middle-aged man and his attractive daughter sitting next to Ithel ap Robert?'

'Yes, I think I know who you mean.' I made a great effort to sound casual.

'That man is probably the most important man you have ever shared a meal with. His name is David Hanmer of Hanmer Hall, and he is a leading lawyer, highly thought-of by King Richard and many powerful lords in London. There is talk that he will soon be appointed a special judge, working exclusively in the King's interest. His daughter is Margaret, or Mared, depending on whether she is addressed in English or in Welsh. She is the wife of Owain ap Gruffudd Fychan, Lord of Glyndyfrdwy and Cynllaith Owain, otherwise known as Owain Glyndŵr. You did yourself no harm tonight as far as those two are concerned. They were both visibly moved by your performance.'

I grunted a reply and hurried into my own bedchamber. The news that Mared was already spoken for was a hammer blow, shattering my foolish hopes and dreams. My mind was in a state of total confusion and my emotions, having been excited out of all proportion and common sense during that wonderful evening, were thrown into deep despair. I did not bother to undress for bed. Instead I sat in an armchair unable to tear my thoughts away from Mared Glyndŵr, knowing full well that the gift of sleep would not be mine that night.

Iolo's prediction of an increase in invitations to entertain the local lords and barons proved correct. Following the success of that first evening at the home of Archdeacon ap Robert, we were kept very busy spending weeks, sometimes months, on end, away from the cosy stone cottage at Coed y Pantwn.

Eventually the call came to attend the young Owain ap Gruffudd Fychan, Lord of Glyndyfrdwy and Cynllaith Owain, at his main hall in Sycharth, some seven miles south-west of Oswestry. Iolo was excited at the prospect of introducing me, his kinsman and disciple, to Glyndŵr and I have to confess to feeling a trifle nervous. I knew that he was a tall, well-muscled young man, very athletic and already a champion jouster. He had also just completed seven years at the Inns of Court in London, where young men of substance were taught English law as well as politics and good manners, including how to acquit themselves in illustrious company such as at the royal court. Iolo, who had known him since childhood, was particularly keen to see how the young man had benefited from such a privileged education, obtained, of course, through the influence of his father-in-law, David Hanmer.

2

EVEN IOLO'S RICH descriptions had not prepared me for
my first sight of Sycharth. It was simply breathtaking.
We had been walking up a wooded slope on a fine spring
morning. The whole area under the trees was awash with
bluebells nodding their heads gently in a slight breeze with
the dew glistening on their swaying leaves.

We were still savouring the sight when we reached the
top of the hill, emerging from woodland to cultivated land
and our first glimpse of Sycharth's splendour. The moated
dwelling stood on the far side of a shallow valley, and on
the sloping meadow leading down into the depression long-
horned cattle were grazing. Iolo was later to write a beautiful
poem describing Glyndŵr's home in accurate detail. When
I read that poem, I realised that some can paint a picture in
words every bit as realistically and artistically as the artist's
brush.

It was a timber-framed house raised on top of a
motte and its surrounding bailey. To my kinsman it was
a 'baron's court, much frequented by bards, the best place
in the world'. He described it as being 'girdled by its moat
of shining water', with a bridge and a 'lordly gatehouse'
leading to a 'fair wooden house on the crest of a green
hill upon four wondrous pillars'. Iolo claimed it to be 'as
high as Westminster cloisters'. It also had a slated roof
and 'a chimney which dispersed smoke'. Within its private
chambers he listed the nine wardrobes full of rich clothes

and other treasures, 'each like a well-stocked shop in London's Cheapside'.

It had a number of stained-glass windows which Iolo thought comparable to those of St Patrick's Church in Dublin. Close at hand were a church, stables, a pigeon house, a deer park, orchards, a fish pond, rabbit warren and heronry, while all around lay 'smiling green meadows and hayfields and neatly cultivated cornfields'. To cap it all, and I can vouch for the truth of Iolo's assertion, the welcome at Sycharth's inviting hearth was always generous and warm.

That first evening of entertainment was to see Iolo like a man inspired. The dining hall was full for the evening meal. Owain sat at the head of the host's table with the frail figure of his mother, the Lady Elen, at his side. Mared was away visiting her family at Hanmer Hall. The company included several of the seneschals who managed Owain's estates on the banks of the river Dee and in Cynllaith Owain, as well as visiting members of the Glyndŵr family. Among them were Owain's recently wedded younger sister, Lowri, and her husband Robert Puleston, son of a powerful landowning family with estates in Cheshire, Shropshire and Flintshire. Also seated at the top table were Owain's brother, Tudur, Lord of Gwyddelwern, and his wife.

Iolo chose the occasion to perform a new poem for the first time. In a preamble, he reminded his audience that the previous year, 1382, marked one hundred years since the last native Prince of Wales, Llywelyn ap Gruffudd, had been ambushed and killed by the English, enabling Edward I to take direct control of all of Wales beyond the Marches. He then sang his new poem, dedicated to Owain ap Thomas ap Rhodri, popularly known as Owain Lawgoch, or Owain of the Red Hand. Though brought up in England,

Owain Lawgoch was very aware that he was the grandson of Rhodri ap Gruffudd, one of the late Prince Llywelyn's brothers and, therefore, the last direct male descendant of the royal house of Gwynedd and genuine claimant to the title, *Tywysog Cymru*, or Prince of Wales. He had spent most of his adult life as a mercenary and adventurer, leading a largely Welsh mercenary force in the service of the King of France. In the 1370s he formally asked the French King to support him in an attempt to drive the English out of Wales and re-establish the House of Gwynedd's pre-eminence, with himself as Prince of Wales. The English authorities were very concerned when they learned of this. It was one problem they could do without and ruthless action was required. Sometime in 1378, Owain Lawgoch was stabbed to death in France by an English assassin, while he slept. Iolo's poetic version was, of course, a heart-rending and greatly embellished account, extracting the maximum emotion and empathy from his listeners. The wily old rascal allowed the final note to degenerate into a deep sob. The audience went wild, clapping, shouting plaudits and banging on tables for a full five minutes. My crafty kinsman had chosen his audience very carefully for the poem's first performance. Among the *uchelwyr*, genealogy was of great importance, and everyone in Sycharth that evening knew full well that after the death of Owain Lawgoch, there was only one Welshman who could claim the title Prince of Wales; only one who was a descendant of all three main royal houses of Wales – Gwynedd, Powys and Deheubarth, and that was their own Owain Glyndŵr.

However, there was no serious thought being given to any form of rebellion in Wales at the time. While the homage paid to Owain by the bards was genuine enough, the idea that the

Welsh would, or could, rise up and drive the English out of their country was still the stuff of legend, myth and ancient prophecy. In any case, was Glyndŵr not one of the most respected among the squirearchy of the March and a solid establishment figure, having married into one of the most prestigious Anglo-Welsh families, with close connections to the English King Richard II? He was also to embark, for most of the 1380s, on successive periods of military service in King Richard's armies.

When the evening's entertainment was finally over, Owain came across to congratulate Iolo on his tribute to Owain Lawgoch. Seeing him approach, I hurriedly stood up and bowed deeply. It was the first time we had met.

'Well, Iolo... is this young giant the kinsman you promised to bring with you?'

'He is indeed, my lord.' Iolo bowed solicitously, his black robes studded with stars and cyphers rustling on the flagstones as he did so. 'I gave him the night off tonight, but when next it is your pleasure to be entertained he will be delighted to sing for you, will you not, Gruffudd... Am I correct in thinking that the Lady Mared will be home by Friday evening? She has already heard the young man in concert and was much affected by his performance, even to the extent of shedding a tear or two...' the old rascal added, his rheumy eyes glinting mischievously.

'My uncle exaggerates, my lord,' I volunteered nervously. At that moment I could have strangled the old goat with his tangled beard.

Owain laughed aloud. 'I see you still enjoy taking every opportunity to try and cause mischief, Iolo.' He turned to me, his unusual golden eyes still friendly and smiling. 'Don't worry, Gruffudd. I know your uncle of old and we both enjoy some hearty leg-pulling when the chance arises. But let us talk of you. You are still a young lad, but you are one of the few men I have met who are a head taller than me. You have the physique to be a mighty warrior. Have you ever been trained in the use of weapons?'

'No, I have not, sire. I may be big but I would probably be too slow and clumsy to be of any use as a soldier.'

'I do not believe that for a moment. Plenty of exercise and practice would sharpen you up significantly. Join me in the practice yard tomorrow at ten.' He gave me a friendly clap on the shoulder, before marching briskly out of the hall.

I turned to vent my spleen on Iolo, only to find that he had craftily sidled away and was standing by the fireplace, talking animatedly to a young serving maid with attractive chestnut hair. Whatever he was saying was making the girl laugh and blush alternately. Surely, she would not agree to whatever perverse nonsense he was suggesting to her? Suddenly she turned and walked to the servants' door. Well done, I thought, she had put the old lecher in his place. Then, to my utter astonishment, she turned in the doorway, grinned and gave him a knowing wink, before disappearing down the corridor. The renowned bard turned to me, a slow gratified smile spreading across his wrinkled face. Then with a quick, triumphant wink of his own, he too hurried out through the servants' door.

The following morning's foray into Owain's world of weaponry was not a happy one for me. My attempts at handling sword and pike were even less successful than I had feared. Owain was a very patient instructor but after several hours of effort, even he began to lose his optimism regarding my potential as a warrior.

'I'm sorry, lad,' he sighed at last. 'Thanks for trying so hard, but I think we both know now that you are neither a natural swordsman nor a promising pikeman. Never mind, tomorrow we will see how you fare with a longbow. You certainly have the strength in your arm and shoulder to draw the biggest bow. The trick will be to teach you.'

The next day, Owain brought his brother, Tudur, with him. I had never seen the two standing together before. They looked so alike they could easily have been mistaken for twins. Closer scrutiny revealed Tudur to be about two inches shorter than his brother and he did not possess Owain's distinctive golden eyes. Tudur had brown eyes, but the same shock of light brown, blond-streaked hair. Even his beard was fashionably forked, like Owain's. The only other facial distinction I noticed was the small mole under Owain's left eye, which was absent from Tudur's face.

'Morning, Gruffudd. I've brought my brother along because he is an expert with the longbow. He will make a much better instructor than me.'

'Good morning, my lords,' I responded. 'I am just worried that you will both be wasting your time. I am no good with delicate skills like combining eyesight and dexterity of the fingers.'

'If your fingers are skilled at plucking the strings of a harp, Gruffudd, then you should be halfway to controlling the trajectory of an arrow as it hurtles from the bowstring,' said Tudur with a smile.

An hour later it had become painfully obvious to the three of us that we were wasting our time. At last Tudur wearily conceded defeat.

'I cannot see how Gruffudd will ever be a soldier without

having the skill to wield some weapon effectively in battle,' he said apologetically.

'I'm sorry, Gruffudd, but nothing I can do will ever make an archer of you, I'm afraid.'

I grinned at him, trying to put on a brave face. 'You have only confirmed what I have always guessed. From now on I shall restrict my fingers to what they do best, and that is to pluck the strings of a harp.'

'Maybe there is a faint hope left for you yet, my young bard,' said Owain suddenly. 'There is one weapon we have not tried – the battleaxe. On the face of it, those big muscular arms and shoulders would be ideal for swinging the axe. You would need to learn the skills to wield it accurately in hand-to-hand combat, of course, in defence as well as attack, and I believe I have the ideal tutor in mind for you. He is a rough, tough sort of man and he will call you all sorts of names all day long. I will wager a gold amulet that he will succeed in transforming our young bard into a deadly axeman.'

'You are thinking of Einion y Fwyall (Einion of the Battleaxe), the blacksmith from Maelor Saesneg,' Tudur laughed. 'I do not possess a gold amulet but I will wager my best silver amulet that Einion will fail. If I lose the wager I will give my amulet, not to you, brother, but to Gruffudd for being such a good sport and for succeeding in becoming a competent axeman.'

Owain looked thoughtful for a moment, a half-smile on his face.

'This may take a few days to arrange, for I will have to summon Einion from Maelor Saesneg and compensate him for loss of earnings while staying with us. Gruffudd, I would advise you to find a battleaxe to your liking in the armoury and spend an hour or two practising your swings. Tudur will show you the rudiments of axe play, then, the more you tune up your muscles for use of the weapon, the less arduous will be your time with Einion, when he arrives. Be aware that he will be a hard taskmaster.' Owain frowned ominously.

I watched the brothers walk away with Tudur chuckling quietly, and my heart sank at the thought of being hassled and chastised for a whole week by some blacksmith who sounded a real bully. I had learned quickly that life was never dull at Sycharth.

My black mood soon lifted when I remembered that it was Friday, and that the Lady Mared would be back at Owain's side for the evening meal and the entertainment to follow.

3

I WAS GETTING ready to go downstairs to the dining hall that evening when there was a hesitant knock on the door to my bed chamber.

'*Dewch i mewn,*' I called solicitously, inviting the person to enter.

The door creaked slightly as it opened to reveal the attractive, chestnut-haired maid I had seen chatting and giggling with Iolo at the end of the entertainment, two nights before. She stood hesitantly on the threshold so I motioned her in, conscious of the long, curling hair like burnished copper arranged with calculated carelessness around her bare shoulders. By all the saints, you had to marvel at how the old lecher could pick them.

'Do sit down,' I said. 'And what is your name?'

She sat on the edge of an armchair, clutching her hands nervously and staring at the floor.

'I am Carys, Master Gruffudd, and I am one of the serving maids. Oh, I do hope you will not think too badly of me but I have come… I have come to ask a great favour of you.'

I sat down slowly on the edge of my bed looking at her appraisingly. This most unexpected of visits intrigued me. What could she possibly want of me?

Carys seemed to be making her mind up about something. She suddenly stood up, straightened her back and approached me. Her new-found confidence made me feel that I should also stand.

'Master Gruffudd... we are both young, but we are grown up and no longer children. I'm sure you will remind me of my place if I sound too forward.'

'No, no, carry on... er... Carys. You obviously need to say something which, to you at least, is of some import. Do feel free to confide in me.'

'Iolo and I...,' she paused, a helpless look in her dark eyes. 'I want you to know that... that Iolo and I are... lovers...' her voice tailed away as if the sheer effort of making the announcement had taken all of her strength.

There was a short silence as both of us struggled to find words to continue the conversation. Carys was standing very close and I was conscious of her femininity as she nervously clutched a long, curling strand of chestnut hair, before drawing it across the fullness of her lips. Her head hardly reached my chest and as she looked up at me, her eyes troubled, I saw how terribly vulnerable she seemed. A strong urge to protect her spread through my whole being. It was only with some difficulty that I resisted the temptation to throw my arms around her and hug her.

She seemed to sense my sympathetic reaction for she grasped my large hand in both her small ones. 'I know how strange this must seem to you because of the huge difference in age between Iolo and me, if nothing else. But he has something which I have yet to find in any other man. He...'

She raised her eyes again and I smiled back at her, my heart beating faster than I wished to admit. And suddenly the words came spilling out of her as if she had at last decided it was all or nothing.

'… well, he seems to have the knack of making a girl feel that while we are together, nothing else matters to him but to please me. And he carries that into our bed too. It's not about him blindly seeking satisfaction with no thought for the woman's needs, as with other men. Oh no; Iolo seems to know every little secret of how to please a woman, and the whole experience is one in which he concentrates on giving pleasure, with little thought for his own gratification. In truth, he seems to carry me from one peak of pleasure to another, then another until we both end up so thrilled and excited it's… just heavenly.'

The frankness of her words embarrassed me and I drew away from her a little.

'Well, Carys, thank you for being so honest and frank. But why are you telling me all this? Forgive me but should what you have told me not be a secret between lovers. I'm not sure I have any right to know such things…'

'Oh yes, Master Gruffudd. There is a reason for confiding in you in this way. You see, having a secret relationship in Sycharth is extremely difficult. Tonight is my one free night of the month. Iolo, rather than perform as the master bard at the end of the evening, wishes to confer that honour upon you, particularly as you have a new poem to perform. This arrangement would allow him to slip away from the hall much earlier to spend time with me.'

'Well, I'll be damned,' I spluttered incredulously. 'So the old schemer sent you to me to do the persuading…'

'Oh please, Master…'

'For goodness sake, Carys, will you stop calling me master. My name is Gruffudd. Now, let me tell you why it is impossible for me to agree to your wishes. Firstly, I am still a novice and lacking in experience. More importantly, the honour of being the highlight of the evening is decided by the host, not by some pompous old bard.'

'Iolo says that all he has to do, is formally ask the host if he would agree to honouring a young poet of promise by granting him the final spot of the evening while he, the holder of that position, volunteers himself for a less prominent role in the entertainment for this one evening.'

'The crafty old schemer,' I exclaimed. 'So in one stroke, he impresses host and guests as the "oh-so-modest leading bard" making "such a selfless gesture" in support of his young protégé. Not only does he enhance his image with the assembled company but, at the same time, gets to bed one of the most attractive maids in Sycharth, a young girl of less than half his age!' The effrontery of the man was almost unbelievable.

Carys smiled at me sweetly. 'Iolo said you would understand.'

And with those words she flounced out of the door, leaving me lost for words.

When I finally entered the dining hall, nerves on edge, Iolo was talking animatedly to the other two bards who would provide supporting performances during the evening. On seeing me he stopped in mid-flow, held his arms out wide and greeted me as if we had not met in years.

'My dear Gruffudd, how good to see you. I hope you are in fine voice for you will be the centre of attention tonight.'

'But you will not be present to support me,' I muttered bitterly.

Before he could reply a page announced the arrival of the host and his party, and the rest of us all stood and clapped them to their seats at the top table.

The remainder of the evening had an unreal quality, almost like a dream. At first I could not take my eyes away from the Lady Mared, seated on Owain's left, while the Lady Elen, his mother, sat to his right. Mared was a vision of loveliness in a pale blue cotton gown with a gossamer shrug thrown around her shoulders, taking my breath away. She spent most of her time speaking animatedly to Owain and trying gamely to bring Elen into their discussion. She had little success, for Elen was now old and frail, and her mind often wandered, leaving her looking vacantly into space. I warmed to Mared, trying so hard to engage the old lady, for it spoke volumes for the kindness of her nature and her generosity of spirit. She was obviously very much in love with her husband and it made her more vivacious and alive than even when I last saw her. It also increased my yearning for her. This, combined with my natural, nervous anticipation due to my elevation in the entertainment programme, caused my stomach to tighten like a knot, making it difficult for me to think and breathe.

After the meal had ended and Owain stood to announce the evening's entertainment, Iolo got up quickly with raised hand. As Carys had predicted, the sly old goat used her very words to me, entreating him to allow me, the best pupil he had ever had the privilege of teaching, to take the final highlight performance of the evening.

Before Owain could answer there was a general murmuring, first of disbelief and then of acclamation, followed by loud hand clapping. After such glowing support for Iolo's suggestion, Owain had little choice but to agree and he did so graciously.

'My friends, you have made it very clear that you approve of the change in the running order of our evening's entertainment. Though I have never heard Gruffudd ap Caradog sing his poetry before, I have already found him a personable young man. The master recommends him strongly and, indeed, there are others here who have heard him and who speak well of him, too.' At this point he looked down at Mared with a smile. 'I am happy to change the order so that Gruffudd ap Caradog will be our master bard for tonight.' He sat and nodded to me with a broad grin as another bout of clapping began.

The first two bards, whose poetic efforts were uninspiring, both made the error of performing for too long, so that the bored audience started murmuring while each bard still sang – a very unusual occurrence. When Iolo started plucking the strings of his fine harp everyone perked up. He had decided to reprise his new poem of praise to Owain Lawgoch which had been such a success earlier in the week. Unfortunately, despite singing it competently with note-perfect harp accompaniment, it was obvious to me, and indeed to anybody who was used to listening to the revered Iolo Goch, that his heart was not in it and he sang the song much faster than previously, with little of the emotion which had elated everyone at the earlier performance. I quickly realised that Iolo's mind was on the delights awaiting him in his bedchamber, and his objective was to finish his contribution to the entertainment as quickly as possible. The applause was sterile rather than enthusiastic, and I could see that Owain was mystified and angry. Mared, like most of the audience, looked very disappointed.

As he stood, Owain switched quickly from a scowl to a warm smile.

'And now we come to the highlight of the evening and it

is time to welcome our newest master bard. My lords, ladies and gentlemen – I give you – Gruffudd ap Caradog.'

As I walked to the centre of the small stage the applause was polite but rather muted. I settled myself on the stool beside my battered old harp, and all I could feel was shame. I imagined how incongruous I must look – a huge man on a small stage, with my physical imperfections anything but poetic – not exactly what they expected in a man they imagined as being musical, sophisticated and gentle. I stole a quick glance at the top table. Mared was sitting with hands clasped, her elbows resting on the table expectant and, was that nervousness I detected? I was aware that my cheeks were burning. Owain was leaning back in his chair, seemingly relaxed, but there was directness in his gaze as if he was willing me to do well. That expression on my host's face settled me. There were two people in the hall, at least, who were wishing and expecting me to do well. My confidence came welling back and as I struck the first chord on the harp I resolved to take my moment and give them a concert they would enjoy.

I began with the sorrowful story of the tragic young girl, which had been so successful at the Archdeacon of St Asaph's home. Again, my mellow baritone voice was in good form and I used it, and the harp strings, to produce the most beautiful notes with simple resonance and warmth of tone, so that they seemed to linger amongst the rafters before slowly dying away. I brought out the stark and complete despair of the young girl as she threw herself into the raging waters of the river, and the utter desolation of her young lover when he perceived the awful finality of her death. The result was beyond my wildest dreams. Every female in the hall, servants as well as guests, was in tears as, indeed, were some of the men. Owain and Mared came hurrying over to me. Throwing away all inhibitions, Mared flung her arms around my neck, and, standing on tiptoe, she whispered in my ear, 'Oh, Gruffudd, I have never heard anything so beautiful. Thank you, thank you.' Then she promptly kissed me on both cheeks.

Now it was Owain's turn as he grasped me roughly by the arms, then shook my hand in a vice-like grip.

'Mared speaks truly, my friend. I, too, have to admit that I have never experienced anything like that performance. You have made a name for yourself this night, and you have saved the evening from being less than ordinary, which I also appreciate very much.'

When the entire hubbub finally died away I introduced my second item and there was a deathly hush, everyone hanging on my words.

'I have composed a new poem which is a tribute to the longbow men of Wales. As you all know, Welsh archers have become feared for being accurate and deadly on battlefields and not only in Wales, but in foreign countries as well. I think it is time for us to honour them and some of their brave deeds. This will be the first public performance of this poem.'

There was loud applause which ended quickly as I drew my first notes from the harp. I had set the words to a popular melody which they all knew. I began with a short introduction, tracing the development of the longbow over the course of several centuries until 1282, when the English King Edward I finally completed the conquest of Wales. This was accomplished when Llywelyn ap Gruffudd was tricked into an ambush in mid Wales, where he and his personal escort were overcome and killed by overwhelming numbers.

Llywelyn's head was severed and sent to London to be placed on public display.

The English had learned over the previous century to respect and fear the Welsh longbow. One of Edward's first actions after completing the conquest of Wales was to investigate the composition and construction of the weapon, so that he could create English companies of similar longbow men for his own armies. The weapon was a large and powerful one often made of ash and sometimes of yew, though the best yew bows were made of imported French yew. It was between six feet and six feet six inches long, and the arrow was a full yard in length. It took tremendous strength to draw the bow properly, and Welsh archers were trained intensively from a very early age with bows made progressively larger as they grew to manhood. I sang of how the strain placed upon the drawing bicep was significant and without being nurtured and hardened to this exercise from childhood, a man learning to use the weapon as an adult could often sustain serious damage to the bicep and shoulder. The longbow had a range of up to three hundred yards and it was lethal, even against the most sophisticated armour, at up to one hundred yards. I then sang of King Edward's decree that a percentage of his soldiers should practice archery for a set number of hours every day, even on Sundays.

Despite his best efforts, Edward found it exceedingly difficult to produce archers of calibre in sufficient numbers. He was therefore delighted to find that large companies of Welsh archers were prepared to serve as mercenaries in his armies. I sang of how, as early as 1298, thousands of Welsh archers fought for King Edward against the Scots at the battle of Falkirk, and made a significant contribution to their victory, despite some serious trouble between the Welsh and the English on the eve of the battle.

Everyone was listening with rapt attention as I went on to sing of how thousands of Welsh longbow men fought with the English at Crécy in 1346 under the distinctive red banner first used by the seventh-century hero Cadwaladr, and again at Poitiers in 1356. They listened with pride as I sang of the significant contributions made by Welsh longbow companies in these battles. I sang of how thousands of Welsh soldiers stripped French fields of leeks and wore them in their caps and helms to ensure that their English comrades would not mistake them for the enemy. This was the beginning of a tradition for Welsh soldiers to wear the leek in battle.

I concluded my song with an account of how at Crécy, it had been the dragon banner of Wales which was thrown over the unconscious body of the Black Prince by Welsh archers, when the sixteen year old was thrown from his horse. They formed a defensive ring around the fallen prince, drawing their short swords to defend him from a ferocious attack by the French and holding out until English men-at-arms arrived, so they could combine to put the French to flight.

After I had sung my final note with a flourish, I was given an even greater reception than for the previous rendering. There was shouting, cheering and clapping for a full ten minutes with few signs of the applause ending until Owain banged the table and raised his other hand for silence.

'Gruffudd ap Caradog, you have given us a wonderful performance of bardic singing at its best. Your work is new, fresh and imaginative and I, like many others here tonight, will remember and treasure that performance for years to come. We began by light-heartedly making you the master bard for one evening at the request of the renowned Iolo Goch. In fact, you sang for us as well as any master bard. I would go so far as to say that this night, the music and poetry you presented to us was the best and most enjoyable I have ever heard. In fact, I am so pleased that I am inviting you to take up a full-time position as resident bard in my household.'

Owain's next words were drowned in a sea of acclaim and he had to wait several minutes before he could continue. For my part, I was looking around the hall in disbelief, wondering whether I was dreaming or not. What I was being offered was beyond my wildest dreams. It would be a safe, pleasant life, well paid, with meals and a roof over my head in comfortable surroundings, in return for work which I enjoyed. With these words he turned his attention to the applauding guests, thanked them for their presence, hoped they had enjoyed themselves and bid them good night. As he and the Lady Mared turned to leave by the door behind the top table, she turned to me, smiled warmly and gave a little wave before following her husband. All I could manage was a weak smile, for so much good fortune had befallen me in a short space of time that I was still more than a little bemused.

All at once I felt very tired and drained. I made my way upstairs, running a gauntlet of compliments as I left the hall. Passing Iolo's bedchamber I heard some girlish giggling and a short, stifled shriek. So the old goat was still busy entertaining the staff.

Once in my own chamber I prepared for bed and wondered how the great lover would react to the news of Owain's proposal. If I accepted, would he be envious and annoyed with me, or would he be pleased for me. Either way, I had to admit I would miss the old man's company, his wealth of knowledge and his often weird behaviour. My mind was in turmoil yet when I finally placed my head on the goose feather pillow, I quickly drifted into the deep sleep of the virtuous.

As I entered Owain's private quarters the following morning, I was assailed by the wondrous aroma of bacon frying in good, rich animal fat. There was a large iron pan on his log fire. The bacon sizzled as he expertly handled a kind of iron pincers to turn the rashers occasionally. After transferring the bacon onto a pewter platter he cracked several eggs into the bubbling fat and carefully nurtured those before transferring them also onto the platter. It was only then that he turned and greeted me good humouredly, and indicated my seat at the table.

'Well, young Gruffudd, are you well rested after last night's triumph? You transformed the whole evening, lad, from an abject failure into a host's dream. Again, my warmest congratulations. Come, help yourself to some freshly baked bread and plenty of bacon and eggs. I'm cooking for myself this morning so we will not be disturbed. I like cooking for myself occasionally, in any case. Will you have some small beer?'

I tucked into a hearty breakfast for I had been too nervous to eat the night before and was now ravenous. We ate and chatted in relaxed fashion, for Owain was very easy to talk to, especially on a one-to-one basis. He harboured no airs and graces and preferred to talk to you as an equal. There were other occasions, particularly formal ones, when he would expect to be given the respect and deference due to a man of his quality. Otherwise, he had little desire for such treatment and disliked seeing other noblemen expecting, and enjoying, constant deference. He waited until we had both finished breakfast before turning to more serious matters.

'Have you given some thought to the offer I made you last night, to be my full-time retainer as the household bard?' The tawny, tiger eyes were trained on me and I could sense the strength of his personality flowing through them.

'It is a most extraordinary and unexpected honour, my lord,' I replied carefully. 'I truly do not understand why you should choose me for such an honour, for I am hardly past the novice stage. If you had chosen my kinsman I would understand, for his quality as a poet is beyond question, but me...?'

Owain smiled briefly. Then he continued in an earnest tone. 'You really must learn to stop undervaluing yourself. It's almost as if you refuse to believe that you can be good at anything? Whatever else you learn from me, you must believe me when I tell you that you should recognise and accept any talents you have been born with. Let us speak bluntly. I know that the superficial characteristic, which makes you look a little different from other people, concerns you greatly. Well, we all have problems of some kind, Gruffudd. They may be physical or emotional or intellectual, but we must never let them rule our lives. When you recognise the fact that you are already an accomplished poet, a wonderful singer and a natural performer, you will gain the confidence to be better still. By the way, as a natural performer I mean that you know instinctively how to appeal to an audience and how best to present a poem, or a song, in a way which will please the audience. That is a gift my friend, a rare gift which few people possess. My advice to you is, use it and treasure it, for when you perform, they do not see physical imperfections, they can only marvel at the sheer talent and skills that you possess, to present them with an experience which they cannot but enjoy because it touches deep chords in their hearts and in their souls. As for choosing Iolo, I think that would be a disaster. Talented and renowned he may be, but he is an old man and set in his ways. He enjoys visiting the homes of *uchelwyr* for days or weeks and then moving on. Indeed, his presence would soon become onerous if he stayed anywhere for longer – his endless thirst for young flesh would become especially embarrassing to his host. His behaviour last night was unacceptable, for he was even prepared to give a quick, uninspired performance to hurry the moment when he could share his bed with a female servant.'

The yellow eyes flashed as he concluded, and I saw that he was more than a trifle annoyed with Iolo after having been made aware by someone with prying eyes, no doubt, of my kinsman's adventure with young Carys.

I nodded and got up to walk over to the narrow window which overlooked the training yard. 'Is this where you will watch that bully of a blacksmith put me through my paces next week?'

Owain laughed aloud. 'No, I shall do you the courtesy of allowing you three full weeks to get the measure of Einion Fwyall before I even begin to assess you as an axeman. Now off with you to the armoury, and make sure you choose a weapon which suits you. Listen to Tudur's advice for he will know which weapon suits you before you even hold it in your hands.'

The following day, Tudur and I went to the armoury. There

were four different kinds of battleaxes, each type in different sizes. I was drawn to a particularly heavy, wicked looking one. It was a double-headed axe with a short, vicious looking blade pointing outward between the two heads. It had a solid hardwood handle, the whole weapon being chunky and seemingly indestructible.

'The bigger the axe, of course, the heavier – but not so as to cause me any problems,' I enthused. 'The extra weight could be crucial in a contest against a smaller man with a lighter weapon. I would have to make sure that I am skilled and fast in handling it. Also, I feel certain that the added weight of this axe would cause pretty extensive damage even to the finest armour.'

'Well, there you are. You have chosen the best, and a strong man like you should have no problems in handling the extra weight,' Tudur said approvingly. 'All you have to do now is learn all the battleaxe skills from the sweet and kind Einion y Fwyall.'

Tudur rolled his eyes to the heavens and laughed. Then he added, 'I'm still not convinced that you will make an axeman, Gruffudd. You do not have the fire inside you and the thirst to win.' He turned away without looking at me again, and walked away.

His final comments stayed with me all that night and came back, from time to time, to haunt me during the following three weeks. They filled me with indignation, and even anger, that I should be dismissed as a no hoper in my quest to become an axeman. They proved a tremendous help in bolstering my determination to succeed, and to live through all that the cantankerous blacksmith could throw at me – which had been Tudur's intention when he uttered the words, of course…

4

M Y FIRST MEETING with Einion Fwyall on Monday morning was as sudden as it was unexpected. I was stepping out of one of the outer doors of the banqueting hall at the exact moment he was entering. Neither of us, I think, had been expecting anyone coming from the opposite direction and we collided with some force. What annoyed Einion, I suppose, was that he was the one who found himself momentarily moving backwards; no doubt an unusual experience and not to his liking.

'Sorry,' I said cheerily, 'I'm afraid I didn't see you coming.'

Einion's habitual expression was one which seemed to hover on the cusp of a scowl. It was no surprise when I saw the scowl-in-waiting materialise in practised lines across his face. He was a big, powerful man and the angry expression made him look very intimidating. Still, he was a good head shorter than me so I placed hands on hips and smiled at him as nicely as possible. Unimpressed he shouted, 'Why don't you look where you're going, you young fool?'

'Well,' I replied calmly. 'I think it was a case of both of us not paying enough attention to where we were going. Do you not agree, sire?'

He stared threateningly at me for several seconds; then, apparently regaining his self-control, he snorted and pushed passed me without another word. I was out in the yard heading for the training area when I realised, with a groan, that I had just met my new tutor. It had not been the kind of introduction I would have chosen.

Tudur was waiting for me on the training ground. I told him of my short encounter with Einion and he smiled ruefully.

'I'm sorry to hear that, lad. It was not the best way to introduce yourself to a man like him. You will have to work even harder now to win his approval.' Tudur's eyes were drawn to something behind me. 'Ah well, they say the devil often appears if you mention his name. Here he comes. I wish you the best of luck. You will need it.'

Tudur nodded to me and walked briskly towards the menacing figure of the axeman striding across the cobblestones. They greeted each other cordially. They were obviously comrades in arms of long standing. They conversed briefly before Tudur went on his way and Einion called me over.

'Come, my boy, we have wasted too much time already. Let's go over to the barn. We can work there without being disturbed.'

'Shall I get my axe first?'

'No, we won't be entrusting you with an axe for the first week or so.'

'We need to work on your speed and reflexes first. I have a strong suspicion that you are unfit, soft, clumsy and slow, with little idea of how to defend yourself in close combat.'

'Surely that is a harsh judgement, is it not?' I muttered, feeling my hackles rise.

'Don't worry, I shall give you plenty of opportunity to prove me wrong. And if I am mistaken, I shall be the first to apologise,' he replied in a matter-of-fact voice.

The barn was a large wood-and-thatch building, its stock

of hay greatly reduced after the long winter when the cattle had to be kept and fed in the cowsheds. Einion grabbed two hay forks, one of which he threw to me. He then began carrying forkloads of hay over to a smooth area of ground just inside the barn doors, and laying it down in generous quantities over an area some twenty feet square. It only took the two of us a few minutes to produce a thick carpet of hay over the designated ground.

Finally, he turned to me with big smile of anticipation and said, 'Right then, my beauty. Let's see what you are made of.' He strode to the centre of the straw area and said casually, 'I want you to put me on my back and hold me there so that I cannot move for at least ten seconds. I, of course, will be endeavouring to do the same to you.'

I looked at him dubiously. 'We are going to wrestle? But what has this to do with wielding a battleaxe?'

'It has everything to do with being a soldier, no matter what your preferred weapon is. A battle, my lad, is a rough, bloody, often cruel fight to the death and your aim is to kill your opponent by any means possible. When that has been done, you concentrate on killing the next one and then the next. How would you cope, do you think, if you were to lose your weapon in the full intensity of battle? Do you think the enemy would allow you to live just because you have no weapon? Of course not. Your only chance would be to grapple with the enemy, bring him to ground and kill him with your bare hands, before grabbing his weapon and fighting on…'

Without warning, Einion sprang at me, grabbed my arm, spun me around and locked his arms under my armpits with his hands clasped tightly behind my neck. He forced me to my knees and in a blur of movement readjusted his hold so that my head was twisted sideways in an excruciatingly painful grip. I found that struggling only increased the pain, so I stopped struggling.

'At least,' he gasped, 'at least you've got the good sense to know when you are in an impossible situation. You are wise to be still for I need only give one quick twist in this position and your neck would be broken. So, if I had lost my weapon in a real battle but managed to get you into this position, you would be a dead man by now.'

He let go and took a step back while I gingerly moved my head slowly from side to side. There was some discomfort but nothing approaching the agonising pain I had experienced in the ruffian's grip. Then, I stood up to face him once more, readying myself for whatever further pain he was going to inflict on me. Einion's face carried none of the triumphant expressions I had expected to see, now he had bested me. In fact, his eyes were almost friendly as he watched me preparing myself for his next onslaught.

'No, you can relax for a few minutes. We need to talk to make sure that we understand each other. Let's sit down a moment.'

We sat in the comfort of some loose hay and Einion began to describe to me the requirements of a soldier's dangerous life. I sat there, my neck still aching, and listened to the voice of experience, and as he talked I began to understand how fitness and intensive training in close quarter combat were essential if I was to have any chance of survival on the battlefield. Within half an hour my respect for the man had increased immensely.

The remainder of the day was spent in bouts of mock wrestling while he taught me a variety of moves and holds and blows designed to kill an opponent. It was a sobering experience, and I swiftly realised how vulnerable I was. Much as I hated the thought of killing a fellow human being, I resolved to learn as much from Einion as I could. His brutal but effective skills could well save my life in a tight corner.

The following weeks were a gruelling period of intense physical activity. Every morning we would leave Sycharth for a run of some four miles. Though neither of us was built for running, Einion was a surprisingly good runner and very fit. To begin with I found the run totally exhausting and on our return I was good for nothing for at least half an hour. Meanwhile, the blacksmith would be cursing me and champing at the bit to get started on throwing me around and clamping me in painful holds, in the barn. Gradually, my fitness improved and as I got fitter the run became easier, and eventually an enjoyable experience. Also, the wrestling became more competitive as Master Einion discovered that his pupil was developing into a worthy opponent. My reflexes and movement generally had speeded up to a level which Einion admitted was greater than he had expected, and occasionally I would catch the master in one of his own much vaunted holds, causing him pain and annoyance. With the increased fitness I was able to utilise my strength much more effectively, and eventually my greater strength became the deciding factor as I matched Einion in skill and fitness.

Our battleaxe training began with the use of axe handles, weighted on the ends with goatskin bags, part-filled with sand. Einion explained that full-on exercises with real axes were too dangerous. Tudur had already shown me the rudiments of axe play, but the blacksmith's skills in displaying various controlled attacking swings and swift defensive blocking were unbelievable. Again, I was faced with a long and hard road to master the use of the vicious weapon. All the moves were then repeated with real axes, but with all the moves done in slow motion.

Finally, the morning arrived when Einion pronounced that he had taught me all he knew. We shook hands and I thanked him for all he had done for me.

'You are a fine lad, Gruffudd, and I am proud of you. Technically, you are now ready for battle. We will not know how good you are until you are tested in real action. It is only in the forge of battle that champions are made or broken. My belief is that you will be a fearsome axeman, and a very professional soldier, when the time comes. Be sure to keep working at your fitness though, and keep to a regular morning run. You never know when a demand for your services as a soldier will arise. Sometimes the need for military action can come along quite suddenly and unexpectedly.'

Then, he clapped me on the back, placed his arm around my shoulders in a quite uncharacteristic gesture, and marched me over to Owain's private quarters where both Owain and Tudur were expecting us. As we strode into Owain's sitting room we saw that the brothers were seated on either side of the fire. Tudur jumped to his feet, rushed over to Owain shouting in mock fear, 'Owain, look out, look out, the axemen are coming!'

We both stopped, unsure of ourselves, causing Tudur much merriment. Owain too smiled indulgently.

'Alas, my lord,' Einion said drily. 'I fear your brother has inherited none of your stagecraft. He would soon be removed from any performance I have ever seen...'

Tudur affected a crestfallen expression, and Owain turned to me.

'Well, Gruffudd, Einion gave me a detailed report of your training as axeman and soldier last night. He tells me that you have performed well in excess of his expectations, and he is confident that you have mastered enough skills and knowledge to take the field as a competent axeman. I congratulate you and wish you well. Not only are you now our resident bard but also one of my axemen in time of strife. I would now like to appoint you the Lady Mared's champion, guarding her with your life when I am absent from Sycharth.'

I looked at him in astonishment, at a loss for words. Einion nudged me in the ribs.

'I... er... I thank you... thank you, my lord. That is the greatest honour you could bestow on me. I shall guard the lady with my life.'

The golden yellow eyes studied my face for a long moment. 'Yes, Gruffudd, I believe you would. I have chosen you for that very reason,' he said finally before adding, with a grin, 'And now Tudur has something to say. I believe it is to acknowledge the loss of a wager... something which he has no great fondness for.'

'You will remember that I wagered my best silver amulet to you, Gruffudd, if I was proved wrong in my belief that Einion would fail in his attempt to make a soldier of you.'

He looked at me sorrowfully. 'And as a man of his word I must now hand over my prized amulet.'

Then, with a smile he shook my hand and handed me a leather pouch. I opened the pouch and drew out a burnished, beautifully fashioned silver amulet inscribed in Welsh with the words '*Bydd ddewr, bydd ffyddlon, bydd Gymro*' (Be brave, be faithful, be a Welshman).

'Always wear it and be true to the inscribed words Gruffudd, and it will bring you honour and peace of mind for all of your days.'

5

THE YEARS FROM 1384 to the end of the century were the happiest of my life. Living at Sycharth and for parts of the year at Owain's other residence, the fine hunting lodge at Glyndyfrdwy, situated on the banks of the River Dee, it was a time of peace and relative security. Many Welsh labourers, unfree serfs and even the better-off freemen, suffered terribly through the greed of the King and the Lords of the March, being burdened with ever increasing taxes, a total lack of legal rights, and suffering from sporadic yet fatal attacks of the plague. However, many *uchelwyr* like Owain Glyndŵr did rather well from military campaigns in Richard II's armies against the Scots and the French between 1384 and 1390.

In the spring of 1384, Owain, together with his brother Tudur, his friend the 'prophet', Crach Ffinnant and other friends and relatives, formed part of King Richard's army in Scotland. Owain's company, under the command of the notable Welsh warrior, Sir Gregory Sais, were charged with defending the Northumbrian town of Berwick-upon-Tweed, the northernmost town in England, a mere two miles south of the Scottish border. This was the beginning of a period in which Owain experienced the full reality of war. It was also his opportunity to see the practical application of military tactics, how battle plans had to be carefully thought out in relation to features such as local geography, the prevailing weather and the relative sizes and capabilities of opposing armies. It was also the time when he and the Lady Mared started what was eventually to become a large family. When Owain left for Berwick-upon-Tweed he already knew that Mared had conceived their first child. When he returned home, months later, it was to greet his wife and their first-born son.

On the night she gave birth, the Lady Mared was attended by a local midwife, an elderly woman called Malen yr Hendre. Malen was an experienced midwife, having delivered many babies over the years. However, she was now as deaf as a post, with poor eyesight and no longer the bustling, confident midwife of old. After several hours of labour, a panic-stricken maid came running to me from Mared's chamber to report that the birth was not going well. The lady was in great pain and was asking for me. Malen was ignoring her pleas, being firmly against the presence of any man in the birthing room. The situation was not to my liking and in Owain's absence I decided to call in Ednyfed ap Siôn, the man recognised as the best physician in the area. In the meantime, I decided to brave Malen's wrath and go to the Lady Mared to try and give her some reassurance until the physician arrived.

It was very hot and dark in the bed chamber, the window was closed and shuttered and there was a blazing log fire in the hearth despite the balmy late summer weather. Mared looked flushed and as I drew closer I could see that her face was bathed in sweat. She was obviously in great pain. The chamber was full of women, apparently doing little other than wringing their hands, with Malen presiding over the scene sitting on a stool and humming contentedly to herself. When she saw me she stood up shakily and started screaming at me to leave the chamber. I turned on her furiously, hardly believing that my lady could be in the hands of such a charlatan.

'Silence, old woman, or I shall have you thrown out of the chamber here and now,' I thundered.

The anger in my voice cowed her and she stopped screeching at me but continued to mutter darkly under her breath. I turned to the seven female servants of varying degrees surrounding the bed, ordered five of them out of the chamber and told the other two to douse the fire and open the window, to allow some fresh air in. They looked at me dubiously but did as they were told. I then turned to the dear lady and informed her quietly that I had sent for Ednyfed ap Siôn, and, using the most comforting words I could find, asked her to try and relax for a while, assuring her that Ednyfed would be with us in a very short time. I sat on a stool at the head of her bed. She turned towards me, her usually lustrous black hair lank with sweat while her lovely dark eyes gazed directly into mine.

'Thank you, Gruffudd,' she whispered. 'I was so frightened, but now that you are here I feel much safer.'

She smiled wanly through her pain and held out her hand for me to hold in mine.

I thrilled to the touch of my beloved and could have wept with happiness, knowing that she was placing her complete trust in me. After a while she drifted off to sleep, while I held her dainty hand in my large paw, and prayed to Saint David that she and the babe within her would get through the birthing safely. Half an hour later she awoke with a start. The pains had begun again and she groaned as she released her hand and held it against her distended belly, her legs writhing under the blanket.

'Oh, Gruffudd,' she moaned. 'How much longer will we have to wait for the physician?'

I stared in despair across the room at Malen who had long since fallen asleep in her chair by the window. We could look for little help from that quarter. As my lady's pains increased in severity and frequency I began to pace around the room, fighting the rising panic within me, while the two maids comforted her the best they could.

Another hour passed before Ednyfed ap Siôn arrived. He was a tall, thin, middle-aged man with a long scar disfiguring one side of his face. He was something of a hero to many in north Wales, having been captured and enslaved by the Moors off the coast of Spain as a young man. The hideous scar on his face was attributed to a Moorish scimitar which nearly killed him when he resisted the attack on the merchant ship in which he was sailing to the Holy Land, to learn the advanced arts of eastern physicians. Fortunately, his life was saved by the personal physician of the Caliph commanding the Moorish fleet. When he heard of Ednyfed's intense interest in the healing arts, the Moorish physician made him his personal assistant. After many years as pupil and assistant to Mustafa al Rachid, Ednyfed eventually regained his freedom, after nursing Mustafa back to health following a fall from a horse. Mustafa gave him a considerable amount of gold coin to pay for his loyal service and Ednyfed was able to pay for a comfortable berth when he voyaged first on a Moorish vessel back to Spain, then on a merchant ship to London. After practising as a physician in London for a few years he eventually returned to his home in north Wales, where he still had relatives.

Ednyfed took in the situation in the birthing chamber

immediately. His first act was to order the elderly midwife out of the room. Malen would not go quietly and roundly cursed the doctor as she was shepherded out of the chamber by the two maids. Ednyfed ignored her and turned to the Lady Mared.

'Greetings, my lady, and apologies for taking so long to arrive, but it was unavoidable I'm afraid.' He smiled at her encouragingly before adding, 'It seems you have started without me.'

Mared bravely returned his smile, her face again bathed in sweat. 'It is my first child, Doctor... I am not sure what to expect and... the pain has been intense for quite a time now.' For a brief moment her fear and trepidation showed clearly, but she gamely forced a smile again.

Ednyfed looked down at her, frowned and turned to me. 'You must be Gruffudd Fychan. Well, Gruffudd, I'm going to have to examine the patient now so I must ask you to leave to preserve the lady's modesty.'

Before I could move a muscle she reached out and grabbed hold of my hand.

'No!' Her voice was sharp and brooked no argument. Then she continued in a calmer voice.

'Gruffudd is my official guard and protector. He is the sweetest, most honest and reliable friend I could have. This is no time for modesty, sire, and I assure you that whatever he has to witness while you administer to me, I will feel no shame in his presence, only warmth and comfort. In the absence of my beloved husband he is the only one I wish to have by my side. You may, of course, summon any female servants you need to assist you.'

'Very well... er... Gruffudd... you may sit there at the head of the bed to offer comfort to my lady. You certainly have spirit and strength of character, Lady Glyndŵr. Those qualities will help you through the next hour or so.'

Ednyfed smiled at her encouragingly again, placing both hands on her belly.

'We have a complication at the moment in that the babe needs to be turned a little. Do not worry; I have delivered babies in similar situations before. We simply need to proceed carefully and gently, taking a little longer to deliver the infant than we would normally. I know the pain can be very severe at times. You must try to breathe deeply but evenly, and try to relax your muscles, apart from the times when I call on you to push to help the babe on its way.'

I had never seen a human birth but I had seen cows and pigs birthing many times, so I had some idea of what was to come. My heart was filled with dread as I thought of all that could go wrong and how females could easily die giving birth when there were 'complications'. I gently squeezed my lady's hand to reassure her and pressed a damp cloth to her fevered brow, my stomach churning in fear of whatever lay ahead.

My concerns proved groundless, for my lady was in the hands of an expert physician. Ednyfed spent nearly two hours coaxing the babe into this world, stopping for short periods only when Mared showed signs of exhaustion. It was an unusually difficult birth but eventually a boy child was delivered, who promptly bawled loudly to let the whole world know that he had arrived. He was rather smaller than expected but whole of limb and with his father's temper.

Later I returned to visit mother and son to find Mared looking drawn but much brighter than she had after giving birth. The little one was sleeping contentedly in the crook of her arm. She greeted me warmly.

'I shall never forget how you comforted me during the worst agonies I have ever experienced,' she whispered. 'Nor will I forget how you dispensed with that useless midwife and got Ednyfed ap Siôn to attend me. I truly believe that without his skills both the babe and I would have died. I shall report your kindness and care to Owain on his return, you can be assured.'

I felt a warm glow of pleasure at her words. At that moment I was the happiest man in all the world.

Then she added, 'I shall call my first-born Gruffudd.'

'In honour of Owain's late father, Gruffudd Fychan,' I murmured.

The dark eyes were deep pools as they turned to me. The corners crinkled as she gave me a small shy smile. 'Others may think that, but what I shall tell Owain is what I tell you now. Our son will be called Gruffudd in honour of the man whose concern and quick thinking saved both the babe's life and mine. That man is Gruffudd ap Caradog.'

With that announcement she closed her eyes, sighed contentedly and soon both mother and infant were breathing evenly – and sleeping peacefully.

6

I WAS OUT on my habitual morning run when Owain returned from military service in the Scottish Borders. I had just crested the hill from which I first saw Sycharth with Iolo Goch. I stopped for a moment to look down the valley towards the large dwelling and its many ancillary buildings, neatly laid out on, and around, a motte on the hill opposite. On starting my descent I heard the sound of horses' hooves in the distance. I stopped again and gazed down the valley waiting for the horsemen to appear. Then the tall figure of Owain emerged from a copse of alder trees at the bottom of the valley, leading a band of some forty riders. Close behind him rode his brother, Tudur, and Crach Ffinnant, Owain's self-styled prophet, and a few others I recognised, though the majority were strangers to me.

The riders slowed to a canter as they neared the entrance to Sycharth and a sleepy guard hurried to open the gates. They had arrived so suddenly that there were very few people around to greet them, though those who were rushed forward to welcome them with shouts of enthusiasm and joy. The noise alerted the whole compound, and after Owain and his men had dismounted, they were soon surrounded by their friends and families, celebrating their safe return.

By the time I arrived the excitement had quietened a little and most of the returned warriors had retired to their various quarters.

'Owain is back,' the guard informed me as I entered the

gateway. Alun Fychan was a short, spare man of few words but a warm smile, who was one of Owain's oldest retainer.

'Safe and unharmed?' I asked.

'Owain yes, he is fine. Sadly, he lost a dozen men in some fierce encounters with the Scots, and of those who did come back there are several who will be doing no more soldiering, I fear. But that is always the way in war. Win or lose, there is always a heavy price to pay.'

'Which is why it should always be the very last resort, Alun, to be avoided if at all possible.'

'True enough. Unfortunately, we live in barbarous times, facing powerful and ambitious lords who are not afraid to stoop to unlawful acts to make us obey, safe within their circle of power and wealth,' Alun replied, shaking his head sorrowfully.

Then I remembered hearing how Alun's son, Eryl, and his family had been driven out of their home and land by Lord Reginald de Grey of Ruthin a few months before and, without Owain's support, would have been destitute. Eryl was now the grateful tenant of a smallholding, well within the boundaries of Owain's lands.

I hurried to my quarters to wash and change my clothing, for I was anxious to see my lord again and hear of his adventures in the Scottish Borders. I found him sitting with the Lady Mared and Tudur in his quarters, dining on an enormous portion of fowl pie, with bread and root vegetables washed down with best Shrewsbury ale. When he saw me in the doorway he rose quickly, marched over and hugged me like a long-lost brother. He beamed at me as I mumbled a few words of welcome.

'It is so good to see you again, my faithful friend. I have just come from the nursery where I held my first-born son and lifted him to my breast. Not that it did much good to our relationship, for he bawled loudly and struggled to be reunited with his mother.'

Owain paused for a moment, the yellow, lion eyes fixed on me, full of gratitude. For once he seemed to hesitate as he searched for words. 'I am reliably informed that it is only through your quick thinking and speedy actions that Mared, and young Gruffudd, survived the birth. For that kindness I shall always be in your debt, Master Bard.'

I have never been quite sure, and it was a long time ago, but I believe I saw a tear in his eye before he coughed a little self-consciously and resumed his seat. I glanced at my lady and saw that her expression was a mixture of admiration and pride, as if she saw me as some kind of hero. Tudur, also, was smiling warmly. It was a proud moment, and I was filled with elation and joy as Mared invited me to join them at table.

Mared and Owain's happiness did not last long and, after a few days, I noticed a coolness between them which had never been evident before. I came upon my lady sitting on a fallen log in the orchard one day. She was sobbing quietly, her shoulders hunched and her face turned away so that she did not see me until I was beside her. She started and dabbed her kerchief to her eyes self-consciously, looking guilty.

'What ails you, my lady?' I asked anxiously, wondering if she were ill.

'Oh nothing... it is nothing...' she murmured unconvincingly.

'My lady, it is clear to me that you are troubled. Would you like to talk about it...? Talking to a friend about your troubles does help, you know,' I offered, kneeling beside her. In truth, her distress was tearing at my heart strings.

Suddenly, she turned to me placing both arms around my neck before burying her face in my chest. She began sobbing uncontrollably. I patted her comfortingly on her back, praying that nobody would enter the orchard to see us in such a compromising position. She cried for several minutes and, despite my concern that we might be observed, I also realised that her sobbing was therapeutic and she might eventually unburden herself to me. She remained with her head on my chest for some moments after the tears had dried. I was intensely conscious of her warm, supple body and longed to encircle her with my arms and hold her tightly, ready to fight to the death if needs be, to protect her and save her from her pain.

Finally, she lifted her head, her long black hair tumbling down around her tear-streaked cheeks and looked up at me, the pain in her fine blue eyes palpable.

'Owain thinks that little Gruffudd is not quite like other children,' her voice broke and she had to pause to compose herself. 'Owain says he cannot tell exactly in what way... but... but there is something missing in our son. Even worse, I can see Owain displaying none of the closeness and the pride you would expect a father to feel. Oh, I know that the babe is not growing as quickly as you would expect, but he is perfect otherwise... I mean he has all his limbs and faculties. Well he does, Gruffudd, does he not?' Her voice rose sharply as she sought my reassurance.

'I am sure he does, my lady. Yes, of course he does,' I added hurriedly. 'What has led Owain to this belief?' I asked after a short silence.

'I have no idea,' she replied bitterly. 'He says he has no

evidence of it… a feeling only. He says it will probably become clearer as the lad grows older.'

'Forgive me asking, my lady, but… how is he with you? I mean, is he still a loving husband? Surely he is not cold towards you?'

She coloured a little and for a moment I thought I had gone too far.

'I am sorry, my lady, I should not have…'

Mared laughed a brittle little laugh. 'No, no. You are my best and closest friend. You must never be afraid to ask questions of me.' She paused a moment.

'Owain is as loving as he ever was. Indeed, he is almost insatiable in our bed. It is as if he cannot wait for me to become pregnant again.' She stared at the ground for a moment and missed the flash of jealous pain which must have clouded my eyes for a moment. But when she looked directly at me there was not a trace of embarrassment in hers, and I realised, feeling relief, but also some regret, that she had no idea of the effect of her answer on me. Owain was obviously the one and only lover for Mared. And that was exactly as it should be.

Mared spoke truly, for Owain went away to serve in at least half a dozen campaigns with King Richard's armies during the Eighties, and each time he came home, he fathered a child.

The Glyndŵr children appeared in rapid succession. After Gruffudd came Catrin, followed by Lowri, Alys, Maredydd, Madog and Marged. Later there were to be several illegitimate ones such as Gwenllian and Ieuan. According to Welsh law, illegitimate children had the same rights and standing as legitimate ones and, characteristically, Owain honoured that law to the letter, and they were all brought up as equals in Sycharth and Glyndyfrdwy. There were yet a few more who claimed to have been fathered by Owain, but most of these claims were made more in hope than in fact.

Soon after Owain's return from Berwick-upon-Tweed, my fellow bards and I realised that he had brought back a rich, new seam of source material for bravery on the battlefield. We were quick to tap into this rich new store to provide fresh and exciting tales to recount in poems to supplement our library of heroic legends and folklore. I had already sung Owain's praises based on his successful showing in tournaments. I had described him as being 'resplendent in gold and scarlet trappings of the finest kind... fighting in tournaments, shattering men's bodies and overthrowing a hundred knights'. Now I could expand that theme to his exploits on the battlefield.

I never heard Owain mention these exploits. They were tales recounted by his comrades and, no doubt, expanded and subjected to exaggeration with the telling. Still, the similarity of these events as retold by different members of his retinue, at different times and to different audiences, showed clearly that young Owain had made a big impression on his fellows on the battlefield.

The following year, Owain again served in King Richard II's army in Scotland and came to prominence once more for his actions in battle. This time he was accompanied by Tudur; John Hanmer, one of Mared's brothers; Einion of the Battleaxe and Owain's brother-in-law, Robert Pulstone. I, too, would have been co-opted were it not for my role as my lady's bodyguard. Two years later, Owain gained one of the greatest experiences of his life when he served under the Earl of Arundel against the French. He was well known to the Earl and his family. Gruffudd Fychan, Owain's father had held the stewardship of a large area of Arundel land. After Gruffudd Fychan's death Owain's mother, Elen, had sent him to serve as a squire to the Marcher Lord. This campaign finally achieved success when a section of Arundel's army boarded warships to challenge the French in the English Channel. Owain was a member of the Earl's personal retinue, and was directly involved in the action at sea in which the French fleet was defeated.

By 1390 Owain had gained considerable experience of warfare on land and sea. Perhaps even more importantly, he had done so in the company of many of England's leading political and military figures, and had understood the English ruling class's view of the world. He had also noticed their proud awareness and support for England's growing political and military power, and the ultimate aspiration to be the pre-eminent power in Europe. All this knowledge was to prove invaluable to him in the conflagration which erupted ten years later, as I was to find out through personal experience.

But for now all that was in the future and nobody, including Owain, had the faintest idea of the long and arduous struggle to come.

7

T HE CLOSING YEARS of the fourteenth century were tumultuous and disturbing ones in Wales and in England. For a long time Richard II had shown himself a headstrong and irresponsible King. In 1397 he dispossessed Marcher Lords and his most dangerous opponents – Thomas, Duke of Gloucester; the Earl of Warwick; and Owain's neighbour, under whom he had fought in the sea battle against the French ten years before, the Earl of Arundel. Not content with this, Richard had Warwick and Arundel put to death. Coinciding with these events another two powerful Marcher Lords, both with royal blood in their veins – Roger Mortimer, Earl of March and John of Gaunt, Duke of Lancaster – died. The March had never seen such an upheaval in its administrative and leadership structure. At the same time, Richard embarked upon a style of arbitrary rule which, though not illegal, was certainly contrary to recent custom. Against bitter opposition he forced through a succession of heavy taxes and interfered with local government and justice. He began installing his favourites in place of the lords he had dispossessed, and banished more aristocrats who had incurred his displeasure. Among those banished in 1398 was his cousin, Henry Bolingbroke, son of John of Gaunt. This was the greatest of his mistakes and it was soon to prove a fatal one.

In the same year, the Irish, under Art MacMurrough, rose in rebellion and Richard had little choice but to take an army to Ireland to put down the rebels. Seizing on a moment when Richard was embroiled in military confrontation with the Irish, Henry Bolingbroke, or Henry of Lancaster as he wished to be known, landed on the north-east coast of England with an army of his own and marched south to reclaim his rights, gathering strength as he went, for many were ready to support anyone who could offer a credible challenge to the unpopular Richard.

The King hurried back from Ireland, landing in south Wales and making his way to Flint Castle, confident of the support he would receive in his main areas of popularity, north Wales and Chester. He was shocked when he received only minimal support and most of his army melted away, leaving him with no alternative but to surrender to his enemies. He was taken prisoner and deposed before being imprisoned in Pontefract Castle. By the end of January 1400 he was dead. Some say he had been murdered on Henry's orders, others that he had been allowed to starve himself to death. The truth will never be known, for no one was ever allowed to see Richard's dead body. May God grant him rest.

The Nineties, in the main, had been kind to Owain Glyndŵr. He had enjoyed a lengthy period of peace and stability in his role as a Welsh aristocratic landowner with the time and freedom to make his home, in the words of Iolo Goch, 'a place of bards'.

However, in addition to his largesse to bards and minstrels, he had made great efforts to improve the lot of the people who inhabited his estates. He was held in the highest esteem by all who lived on his lands for he was a fair and sympathetic landowner, quick to see genuine examples of real poverty when he would invariably step in to help. He was also a devoted father and, by the end of the century, his 'brood of chieftains' had increased to thirteen, at least five of whom were not Mared's. He was certainly not the perfect husband, and was often tempted by a shapely female ankle flashed deliberately to draw his attention, for Owain was a handsome man even in his middle years. Yet, somehow, his relationship with Mared, after some rocky moments, held together remarkably well. Mared, for her part, knew that whichever ankle tempted her man, it was never anything other than a transitory physical attraction. When she spurned him, Owain would endure days, sometimes weeks of emotional hell until Mared forgave him, for she was his one true love and she knew it. Yet I, alone, knew of the pain and disappointment my lady suffered through Owain's thoughtless philandering.

Thanks to the Earl of Arundel and the Hanmer family, Owain had been able to live and study in London, mix in aristocratic English circles and to visit the King's court, getting to know Richard, the Boy King, and many courtiers and other men of standing. He had naturally assumed that he would progress in those circles. After distinguishing himself on the battlefield, I think he hoped for a knighthood or possibly some important role, representing the English monarch in his native land. None of this had come to pass, but still he was seen by the English as a safe pair of hands and an establishment man they could rely upon in Wales. What they did not take into account was his royal Welsh ancestry, his deep awareness of, and pride in his royal position, and his anger because of the terrible and increasing suffering of his people due to English greed and insistence on governing the Welsh as second-class citizens, with no rights in law. When poets, myself included, sang of the proud and powerful people from whom we are descended, and the large area of Britain we had ruled and converted to Christianity following the withdrawal of the Romans, they had no conception of how such tales could stir the flames in the heart of a man like Glyndŵr.

They were almost certainly unaware of the legend of *Y Mab Darogan*, the Son of Prophecy, which had been at the root of Welsh dreams of a return to former glories for centuries, and which promised that a warrior would one day appear, in some versions called Owain. This was a leader who would deliver the Welsh from servitude to the English and recover the crown of London for its rightful owners, the Britons, now called the *Cymry*, or as the English would have it, the Welsh. And even if they had been aware of the legend, there is no way they would have understood its intense significance for Owain. Neither would they have imagined that the last remaining male descendant of the royal houses of Wales would be tempted, against all the odds, and be prepared to give up his wealth and standing, his precious family, his home as well as risking his own and thousands of other lives – to live the legend. It meant taking on the immensely more powerful, wealthier and twelve times more numerous English, in all-out war. The very idea that such a war could take place would have been ridiculed by the English and by many of the Welsh.

The Welsh *uchelwyr* regarded Henry Bolingbroke as a usurper of the English crown, a view shared by many in England. Henry IV's position on that throne was a shaky one. Owain and many others amongst the *uchelwyr* were aware of this. Also, it was generally accepted by the Welsh nobility that rebellion could only succeed at a time when an English monarch's hold on his throne was being threatened from within his realm and, at the same time, from other countries. This was such a time, with powerful enemies like the French, as well as the Irish and the Scots taking up arms against him.

In the end, however, it was the greed of a Marcher Lord which would tip the balance and convince Owain that the new King would allow him and his people no redress for any grievances, and that justice for the *Cymry* would only be achieved by force of arms.

My first confrontation with Lord Reginald de Grey de Ruthin took place a year or so before the fall of King Richard. Owain had asked me to join him in a wild boar hunt in some woods near the northern boundaries of his estates. A small stream marked the boundary of Glyndŵr lands beyond the woods, and on the other side was an area of common land comprising some one hundred acres of wet marsh and scrub, inhabited by a few poverty-stricken serfs. On the far side of this common lay the boundary to Lord de Grey's estates, marked by another stream.

The hounds picked up the scent of a boar a short distance from the Glyndŵr boundary stream. Owain and I were accompanied by ten archers, as huntsmen, and a personal guard of six swordsmen. The boar was a wily old gentleman who made straight for the stream hoping, no doubt, that his pursuers would lose his scent. Owain ordered us all across the stream, and after a short hunt up and down the other side of the stream, the hounds picked up the scent once more and led us onto the common, skirting a stinking marsh and on to a copse of tightly packed willows. The boar must have been at the end of his tether because, as we approached the copse, with the hounds baying for blood, the brave old warrior, squealing with rage, emerged from the trees at a gallop, momentarily startling the hounds. Reaching the first hound, the enraged boar bent low and twisted his head sharply upwards. The two massive lower teeth, more tusks than teeth in reality, tore into the doomed victim's stomach throwing him into the air, his belly ripped open, guts and blood spewing out of him as he screamed in terminal agony. The remaining eleven hounds were onto the boar in a flash and after five gory minutes the creature lay prostrate, unseeing eyes staring, dull and lifeless. Owain called off the hounds, several of whom were now limping and nursing a variety of wounds while Coch y Rhedyn, the pack leader, lay dead.

The hunters had dismounted and were unsheathing their skinning knives when we heard the unmistakable, muffled drumming of horses' hooves on the soft turf before a large party of about fifty armed riders bore down on us. We hastily took up defensive positions, the archers swiftly and expertly stringing their bows and notching arrows in readiness while the guard unsheathed their swords and lined up alongside Owain, who remained calm and did not draw his sword.

The newcomers were led by a short man encased in full body armour, including a helm sporting a showy peacock feather. All the other riders also wore full body armour and were comprised of swordsmen, archers and some armed with pikes. I quietly loosened the string holding fast my battleaxe within its protective leather sleeve. The strangers looked belligerent, outnumbering us by nearly three to one, and I wanted to be ready for swift action.

The short one drew his horse to a halt in front of Owain.

'You disappoint me, Glendower. I had thought you were

of nobler stock than a common thief. Perhaps you would explain why you are stealing wild boar from my lands?' The voice was autocratic and irritating in its haughty tone.

Owain eyed him steadily, and responded in a civil manner.

'Perhaps, My Lord Grey, you would explain what you mean by the words "from my land" when it is obvious to anyone familiar with this locality that we are standing on undisputed common land?'

'Ah, well now, in that you are mistaken, Welshman. As a Marcher Lord I have written to the King pointing out my belief that there should be no such term as common land in conquered territory. All lands within the March should be designated land of the local Marcher Lords, including those previously designated as common land and those presently held on behalf of the King by self-styled Welsh aristocrats, based on tradition and nothing else.'

There were growls of angry dissent from the Welsh party in response to these words. Owain, however, remained silent, but there was a dangerous look in his eye.

'As I have been saying for years, it is high time all Welshmen, of every rank in society, realised that as a conquered race, they have no rights in English law. We issue the commands and whatever we say goes. Your duty is to serve your masters as they shall see fit, and to do as you are told. Now then, Glendower, I see in the midst of those sorry-looking shaggy ponies, an admirable grey warhorse. I have seen you on the battlefield riding that beauty. That is far too good a destrier for a Welshman. I have decided to confiscate it in reparation for your ill-conceived hunt on my land, and for conducting the illegal act of killing a wild boar on my domain.'

Owain turned pale as a barely controlled rage drained his face of blood. I tightened my grip on the handle of my axe, conscious that every member of our party was tensing to attack at the slightest indication from our leader. Then, a slow smile spread across Owain's face. Grey looked puzzled by his reaction, not really knowing what was in Owain's mind.

'By the way,' he added suddenly, 'just in case you are thinking of putting up a fight – be so good as to look behind you before taking any rash decisions.'

I glanced back over my shoulder and swore as I saw a wave of movement from among the willows behind us and a body of archers, some three score in number appeared, forming themselves into two rows, bows at the ready and arrows notched. We were trapped, with fifty or more mounted men facing us and sixty archers cutting us off from the willow copse.

'It would appear, de Grey, that for the moment, you have the upper hand. I have little choice but to bow to your wishes. My steed's name is Llwyd y Bacsie. She is a strong and faithful friend. Treat her well and she will prove the best destrier you will ever possess.'

Owain spoke in a calm but resigned voice, which amazed me. He and Llwyd y Bacsie were the closest man and horse team I had ever witnessed. Each knew, instinctively, the wishes of the other in any situation as if their respective brains were connected by an invisible channel of thought. So, to see him surrender the magnificent destrier so calmly and without an outpouring of impotent rage, at least, was incredible.

'I am glad you appreciate your situation, Glendower.' Reginald de Grey slowly removed his helm, a smirk playing on his florid face. 'I shall treat her as I treat all my horses – with firmness and discipline. I have yet to fail in training a horse to obey my slightest command. The name will have to be changed, of course, I cannot have a horse with an unpronounceable name. She will be known henceforth as Glendower's Gift.' He turned to his men and laughed heartily, and they all laughed with him.

We all glared angrily at the unpleasant creature except for Owain, who simply stared unwaveringly at him, with only the deep contempt in his eyes and a slight clenching of his jaw betraying his true feelings. Then, something strange happened. Llwyd y Bacsie raised her head, stamped her front hoof into the turf a few times, and with a little shake of her head, came trotting over to stand close to Owain. She bent her great neck forward and gently nuzzled her master's chest. Owain patted her jaw and whispered gently in her ear.

'*Da ferch, da ferch.*'

'What magic are you whispering, Welshman?' de Grey snapped accusingly. He swung around in his saddle and beckoned to one of his archers, a bald, middle-aged man who came forward shamefacedly, without glancing in our direction.

'What did Glendower say to the horse?'

The man coughed nervously before murmuring, '*Da ferch, da ferch*, sire.'

'That I heard, idiot! But what does it mean?'

'It means good girl, good girl, my lord,' de Grey's tame Welshman said hurriedly.

'Well now, let's hope she makes the most of it because she will not be hearing any *dah vecks* from me,' the Lord of Ruthin guffawed, his men dutifully emulating him.

'Glendower, I am feeling better disposed towards you, now that you and your little band have understood your place in the scheme of things.'

Without a word, Owain turned away from Llwyd y Bacsie and started walking back towards the Glyndŵr lands. The rest of us followed, also on foot, dejectedly leading our ponies by their reins. Even the hounds seemed dejected as they followed us wearily from the scene. The grey mare whinnied and Owain turned briefly, held up his hand palm forward and turned away once more. The horse stood stock still watching us go, ears positioned slightly forward as if waiting for a signal. Owain, however, kept on walking, heading for the stream. When we eventually forded the stream we turned back to see that de Grey was shadowing us with his band of horsemen, though the three score archers were nowhere to be seen. I guessed they had been sent back to Ruthin. Once across the stream the dejected looking Owain called us over in a markedly crisper manner.

'Get ready for action, lads. If these turds do cross over onto my land we are going to pick them off. Before that though, our friend Reginald, is in for a nasty shock. Now let's walk steadily but not too hurriedly to the cover of the wood. Be sure to maintain your dejected appearance till we get there.'

Once under cover of the trees he ordered two of the swordsmen to take the hounds home to his lodge at Glyndyfrdwy, with a message that the rest of us would come home the following day. Then he gave orders to ready ourselves for action. The ten archers immediately began stringing their longbows. We were only a little more than a hundred yards from the stream, well within bowshot, and we could see the mounted party slowly approaching us. At its head was Reginald de Grey riding Llwyd y Bacsie, again fully armoured having donned his helm with the dashing peacock feather.

'Men, I want you to relax and enjoy the next few minutes. The cocky peacock is about to lose his dignity. Whatever happens, any one of them foolhardy enough to cross the stream is to be skewered like the common robber he is.' Owain's tone was light but I knew him to be in deadly earnest.

The Marcher Lord seemed content and happy with his lot as he rode the striking warhorse. As for Llwyd herself, she seemed the most docile and easily ridden beast anyone could ever hope for. Then I saw Owain cup his hands around his mouth and standing up he performed the most convincing attempt at the poignant two-note cry of the curlew I ever heard. It was a typical bird call in wetlands such as the common we had just left, and which de Grey now claimed as his property, and none of the English riders took any notice of the cry. The effect on the grey destrier was instantaneous and horrifying for the unlucky lord sitting nonchalantly on her back. Without warning, she bucked violently so that de Grey was lifted at least a foot above the saddle to come crashing down again a moment later with unhappy consequences for his more tender parts as they were crushed into the saddle. Llwyd then reared, her front legs pawing the air as the unfortunate lord slid backwards towards her hind quarters. As soon as her front hooves regained contact with the turf she gave a great kick of her rear hooves so that her hindquarters pitched upwards and, notwithstanding the weight of his suit of armour, the great lord was hurled high into the air in ungainly flight well over the horse's head. He landed on his back on the ground with a sickening, clanging sound as some of the armour plating twisted like paper into his ribs, breaking several of them in an instant. His companions stared, transfixed, at their fallen leader. Having momentarily remained silent with the breath knocked out of him, de Grey gave vent to piercing, high pitched screams of agony, as the pain from his broken ribs and a broken left wrist, kicked in with a vengeance. Most of his band rushed forward to assist him but four of them, shouting with rage, spurred their mounts across the stream in the wake of Llwyd y Bacsie who by now was galloping joyously back to her master.

'No one too loose till I give the order,' Owain roared to his archers.

The four English soldiers had now crossed on to Glyndŵr land but Owain waited till the grey was safely back in the cover of the trees before he gave the order to his archers. The foolhardy riders were less than forty yards from the trees when a salvo of arrows from ten longbows went whistling through the air towards them. At that range they might as well have not been wearing armour. The deadly accuracy of the longbows spelled instant death as all four were swept from their saddles and tumbled to the ground to lie still. Each of the ten arrows spelled death to its victim. The lead horseman had four arrows in his chest, any one of which could have killed him.

The other three had been hit by two arrows each, two with a brace in their chests and one in the chest and mouth, the last having smashed his jaw and re-emerged through the back of his head.

Across the stream the others paid little heed to us or their fallen companions, as they struggled to help their hapless leader. Eventually they started to carry the pain-wracked lord homeward on a makeshift bed of tree branches bound together with strips of cloth and covered with cloaks.

After we had secured and tethered the dead men's horses, for they were fine mounts, Owain ordered the four dead men to be buried in unmarked graves. Then, we formed a camp for the night and made do with some bread and cheese for supper, for we had been forced to leave the dead boar behind on the common.

Sometime during the night I was awoken by a call of nature. I got up and signalled to the guard that I was awake and moving around the camp. I suddenly came upon Owain sitting on a fallen tree trunk. He spun around, aware of another's presence even though my barefooted progress towards him had been virtually silent.

'Oh, it is you, Gruffudd.' His tone was friendly but distracted, as if his mind was on something of import.

'Yes, my lord.'

He motioned me to sit beside him. We sat in silence for a long while. His eyes were fixed on the stars and he appeared to have forgotten my presence.

'Are you troubled, sire?' I ventured at last.

'No, no… er… well… yes, I suppose I am,' he raised both hands and ran his fingers several times through his thick mane, looking uncharacteristically hesitant.

'How old do you think I am?' He gave me a quizzical look.

'I know how old you are, Owain.'

'You know, you say. How so?'

'You are in your fortieth year, my lord. It is a bard's business to know such things,' I added quickly. I did not want to admit that the information had been casually imparted by Mared in conversation a few weeks before.

'And you, my loyal friend who has been such a faithful servant and wonderful bard these past thirteen years, you must be about thirty years.'

'I have had the honour of serving you and the Lady Mared these past fifteen years,' I grinned. 'And I shall be thirty-two in two months' time.'

'Then you are old enough to know that certain days in your life stand out in your memory as days of particular significance.'

He paused, his eyes staring directly into mine for several moments. Then he continued quietly, as if talking to himself.

'Sometimes, you are aware of the day's fateful nature immediately, and you can even make plans for adjusting your situation accordingly. There are other times when some instinct tells you that the day is a fateful one in your life, yet there is a dark veil cast over the consequences, which only become apparent at some time in the future. I have a strange feeling, a premonition maybe, that today marks the beginning of a new chapter in my life, perhaps in all our lives. I cannot tell you why for the veil is well and truly cast over the nature of this change. It concerns me, because even though we had a bit of excitement today in our clash with my neighbour, the robber baron, my instinct tells me that this is only the very small beginning of something which will grow into a matter of far greater importance, and which may have untold consequences for us all.'

We both sat in silence for a while. The night suddenly seemed uncommonly cold and we both experienced an involuntary shiver, before the moon slid silently behind a cloud.

8

T HE STORM CLOUDS began to gather over Owain and his fellow *uchelwyr* early in 1399. The accession of the new King, Henry IV, posed a real threat to the very existence of the Welsh nobility. The new Lords of the March had warmed to their newly-acquired lands, and were eagerly looking across their borders at the numerous royal estates held by the Welsh squirearchy in the name of the King. Many of these new lords knew little of the complicated treaties and marriage alliances which Norman and Welsh noble families had entered into for generations. However, they were aware that the usurper Henry Bolingbroke had broken the chain of Plantagenet succession to the English throne, and as the first Lancastrian monarch, had little respect and even less goodwill towards the Welsh barons, the majority of whom had supported Richard II.

None was more avaricious than the Earl de Grey de Ruthin, friend and strong supporter of Henry IV. Even before the demise of Richard II, Grey had laid claim to an area of Glyndŵr land called Croesau in the parish of Bryneglwys, but the case had been found in favour of Glyndŵr. Now, with Henry Bolingbroke on the throne, Lord Grey felt emboldened to seize another portion of Glyndŵr land at Derwen, to the south of Ruthin. My Lord Owain registered his grievances with Parliament several times in 1399 but these pleas were ignored. When Parliament again ignored Owain's renewed pleas the following spring, Bishop

John Trefor of St Asaph, who had been King Richard's ambassador to Scotland, and who would later become one of Owain's most influential followers, warned them it would be unwise to ignore a man of Glyndŵr's stature in Wales. He received the curt reply – 'What care we for barefoot Welsh rascals.'

Instead of having the Derwen lands returned to him, Owain was asked to grant Grey further concessions. He departed from London fuming at the injustices of Parliament and convinced that if he and the other *uchelwyr* were to be fairly dealt with, justice would only be achieved at the point of a sword.

Reginald de Grey was also the King's representative in the northern March. Among his responsibilities was the issuing and enforcing of general musters by the monarch when he wished to raise an army. Local barons were expected to provide a certain number of armed men for the King's army. Henry issued an order to muster an army to fight in Scotland in 1400. The Lord of Ruthin withheld news of the muster from Owain until the very last moment, making sure that he could neither comply with the order nor explain his absence to the King in time. At a stroke, de Grey had ensured that Owain would be deemed guilty of treason, and Bolingbroke would confiscate his lands on his return from Scotland.

It was a crisp autumn morning. Weak but direct shafts of sunlight were making my eyes water as I returned from my morning run to Owain's impressive hunting lodge near Carrog, in Glyndyfrdwy. Keeping myself fit had long become a way of life and now, seventeen years after my initial training as an axeman, it was very rare for me to miss out on my morning run. As I approached the lodge gates a horseman overtook me at the gallop, spraying me with mud from the wet path. Glaring after him I noticed with surprise that his surcoat bore a white lion rampant on a red background, the livery of Reginald de Grey. I had never witnessed a visit to Owain's home from anyone connected with the Lord of Ruthin.

As I entered the cobbled courtyard of the lodge I saw a groom leading the lathered horse over to the stables.

'Whose horse is that, Arwyn?'

'One of Lord Grey's men-at-arms has just arrived with a message for our lord,' the groom responded sleepily as he and the horse disappeared from view.

Later, seated in my quarters struggling for inspiration to compose a new ode, I heard voices speaking English in the courtyard and went to my window in time to see de Grey's messenger mounting his horse and trotting out through the gates. Shortly after, a servant came to summon me to a meeting being convened by Owain. On entering his private sitting room, I saw that several of his chief counsellors were already gathered around the table. Owain bade me sit next to him with Tudur already seated on his other side. Also present were Rhys Gethin, two of Owain's sons – the eldest, Gruffudd, and Maredudd as well as his most trusted captains, Hywel ap Gronw and Ednyfed ap Siôn, who had been retained as the family's private physician ever since Gruffudd's birth, and whose views were valued by my lord on all topics. The last seat was taken by Crach Ffinnant, self-styled prophet to whom Owain often turned for political advice and omens of good fortune. This was a man I had never liked. He had a head of greasy, dark, unkempt hair and his face and hands were covered in scabs and running sores, though it was his personality and demeanour that I disliked, not his physical imperfections. I never understood why Owain laid such store on his views any more than how he seemed oblivious to the man's slyness and self-importance.

'My apologies, gentlemen, for having called this meeting at such short notice.' Owain glanced around the table, his face, split in a small grin, belied by the grim expression in his eyes. I knew that look of old. This was no time for frivolous remarks.

'Most of you will be aware that we had a visitor this morning. It was one of de Grey's men with a message from His Lordship inviting himself here for what was described as a "reconciliation" meeting.' There were incredulous gasps around the table.

'That,' said Hywel ap Gronw with a frown, '… is about as likely as snow in August.'

'And to reassure me,' Owain continued, 'he promised to arrive with no more than thirty armed men so that we could have what he called a "good" discussion to settle our differences. Now this does not sound like the de Grey we know. He is obviously up to something. But what?'

'I smell treachery here.' Hywel ap Gronw spoke with conviction. 'This man has always been one of the most rapacious of lords. Why would he speak of reconciliation now when, only a few months ago, he played the dirtiest of tricks by delaying the King's call to a muster until it was too late for you to comply, ensuring that Bolingbroke will surely outlaw you on his return from Scotland?'

'Why indeed?' Gethin interjected. 'Clearly there is more mischief afoot. My belief is that we should not concern ourselves with De Grey's intentions.' He was interrupted by a chorus of objections but raised his hand for silence. 'Instead let us see this meeting for what it represents for us – a clear opportunity to capture this turd and end his scheming, once and for all.'

'You mean murder him?' Tudur asked, reflecting the shock registered around the table.

'I prefer the word "execute", but to put an end to his treacherous life, certainly,' Rhys confirmed with a wolfish grin.

'No.' Speaking for the first time, Ednyfed ap Siôn's voice cut through the silence like a whiplash. 'That is a base and most unworthy suggestion, Rhys Gethin. Owain is of royal blood and comes from a long line of princes – civilised rulers who followed honourable codes of conduct. No man born into a family of such stature could possibly contemplate making an arrangement to meet an enemy in order to commit cold-blooded murder, no matter how dishonourable that enemy may be.'

Rhys banged his fist on the table, angered by Ednyfed's admonition, and stood up in quick fury as if to leave the chamber.

'Sit down, Rhys.' Owain spoke quietly but with a crisp authority and Rhys Gethin slowly sank back onto his seat, still scowling menacingly at a cool, unperturbed Ednyfed ap Siôn.

'It is impossible to know what de Grey's devious mind has planned for tomorrow but we must be ready for any eventuality,' Owain continued. 'I imagine we can raise a force of sixty or so by tomorrow which gives us a two-to-one advantage over His Lordship. When he and his escort of thirty arrive we will insist that the visitors leave their arms at the gate. Gruffudd, you will lead his men into the dining hall having primed the servants to keep them well supplied with ale. Tudur, you will have charge of our defence force.

You and most of your men will keep out of sight until alerted to any action required. If there is trickery afoot and we need to make a quick getaway, you will pretend to be me and lead your entire mounted force out of the gate heading due south, which should be the least dangerous avenue of escape. There is sufficient family resemblance for you to impersonate me successfully for some time, I'm sure. Rhys, you will take a trusted man with you to look out for any force approaching from the north. Maredudd, you will do likewise to cover the water meadows to the east while you, Hywel, and my son, Gruffudd, will cover the western and southern approaches. If any of you do spot an enemy force, be very careful to stay well hidden. All I want you to do is return to the lodge without being spotted and inform Gruffudd Fychan of what you have seen.' He turned to me with a smile. 'You will come and interrupt my meeting with de Grey and recite a short poem – an *englyn* maybe. Our visitor will not understand a word of it, and even if he did, he would not understand its significance as a warning.'

'But what of you, my lord?' asked Crach Ffinnant in his irritating, fawning tone. 'Who will ensure your safety?'

'My dear Crach, you need not be concerned about my safety,' Owain responded, then turning to me: 'You may rest assured that my burly bard and I will have our own means of escape.'

I looked across at the prophet and saw that his face was twisted in a jealous scowl.

The arrival of the Earl de Ruthin the following morning was colourful rather than threatening. Reginald de Grey, though armed with a sword resting in a jewel encrusted scabbard with matching belt, was not wearing armour. His escort of thirty, likewise, wore no armour and were only lightly armed. Owain met them at the gates with only a dozen lightly armed men, greeting de Grey cordially to his lodge. For his part the great lord was smiling also as he returned greetings in like fashion.

Two years had passed since de Grey had been thrown so violently by the grey warhorse, Llwyd y Bacsie. Now, as he dismounted awkwardly, holding himself stiffly, I could see that his damaged ribs were still causing him a great deal of discomfort when attempting strenuous movement. It made his overtures of friendship towards Owain seem even less credible. I could imagine similar thoughts passing through Owain's mind, though there was no hint of them as he stepped forward to shake de Grey's hand. Without further ceremony, Owain led de Grey away towards his private quarters and a dozen grooms came over to take the horses to the stables. I turned to a short, self-important captain indicating that he should bring his men over to the dining hall for some refreshment, an offer accepted with some enthusiasm by the lord's men.

Much earlier that morning, the eight designated spotters had gone to cover the approaches to the hunting lodge from the four points of the compass. Owain and his guest had only been in conference for some fifteen minutes when Rhys Gethin came running across the forecourt where I was sitting on a stone bench, struggling with my latest ode. Drawing to a halt beside me, Rhys had to catch his breath before gasping, 'As we feared, they mean to kill or capture Owain. Dafydd and I have seen a large body of armed men wearing the de Grey coat of arms marching out of Craigwen woods. There must be two hundred of the bastards.' He looked around wildly. 'Where the hell is Tudur?'

'Calm down, Rhys. We've planned for this kind of

situation. Tudur and his men are waiting down in the orchard. Go down there and join them while I go to warn Owain.' I did my best to sound calm, but my heart was pounding.

'Do it quickly, Gruffudd. They are only twenty minutes away, at most.' Rhys Gethin spun on his heels and raced away in search of Tudur.

I paused outside the door of the small chamber which Owain used as a meeting room at the lodge. I was very conscious of the need to appear relaxed when I delivered the coded message, so as not to arouse suspicion in de Grey's mind. Taking a deep breath I knocked on the door and entered in response to Owain's muffled call. I spoke in English in feigned deference to de Grey.

'I am very sorry to interrupt your meeting, sire,' I said to Owain, 'but I have to go to my sick mother in Carrog right away. I thought you might wish to approve the *englyn* you have asked me to compose for tomorrow's feast. We are unlikely to have any other opportunity to do so.'

Owain turned to de Grey with a pained expression on his face. 'I'm so sorry for this interruption, my lord. But it will only take a minute, with your permission.'

'No need to apologise, my friend. Feel free to listen to the bard's poem,' the Earl responded magnanimously.

'Quickly then, Gruffudd,' said Owain, his tone laced with mock irritation.

I quickly recited the short poem in Welsh. It referred to Dafydd, brother of Prince Llywelyn ap Gruffudd, who was the first man to be hanged, drawn and quartered for treason in 1283 at Shrewsbury, in front of Edward I and the townspeople. It recounted the tale of how, having watched in horror as various parts of his body were thrown into a fire, the agonised prince died. His heart was then torn from his breast and thrown into the flames. Legend recounts how, after sizzling in the flames, the heart hurtled out of the fire into the executioner's face, blinding him instantly and causing severe damage to his features.

Quickly grasping that his life was in immediate danger, Owain turned with apparent calm to his visitor. 'I am not altogether happy with the last line of the poem. Forgive me for a few minutes, Reginald, while I confer on improvement to a few of those words.'

The Marcher Lord smiled again. 'I see you are trained in the bardic art as well, Owain. Carry on by all means. We will have plenty of time to conclude our discussion after.'

We both left the room casually, but as soon as we reached the end of the short corridor leading outside, Owain turned briskly and instructed me to tell him all I knew of the impending danger, while we hurried over to the stables. As we reached the first set of doors there was a shout. Maredudd came racing towards us. I raised my finger to my lips to caution him to silence until we were all inside the stables. I had just informed Owain of the large body of de Grey men approaching from the north. Now Maredudd came bearing more bad news.

'Father, I have just seen a strong force approaching through the water meadows. At first I thought they were de Grey's retainers but then I noticed that their livery sported a red lion on a white background, instead of de Grey's white lion on a red background.'

'Talbot,' Owain snapped. 'That is the livery of Earl Talbot of Chirk. They certainly mean business today, don't they… Get yourself down to the orchard Maredudd, quick as you can, and tell Tudur and his men to leave immediately. You will join them. Tell them to ride south for several miles before heading home to Sycharth. They are, on no account, to attempt to return here. This place will shortly be overrun and I don't want a single armed man left here to face certain death. They are to wait at Sycharth until they hear from me. Is that clear?'

'Yes, Father. But what of you?'

Owain grinned briefly. 'Don't you worry your head about me. The English already believe I am a magician. I shall now fuel that belief further.' He laid his hand on his son's head and gave him a gentle push. 'Now away with you.' He stood for a moment, his gaze troubled but proud as Maredudd ran furiously towards the orchard.

Then he turned to me and said, 'Come, Gruffudd, it is time we took to holy orders.'

I followed him into the dim recesses of the long stables building. In a far corner he opened the door to a tall cupboard. In the semi-darkness I could just make out items of clothing and various solid objects I could not identify in the gloom.

'Quickly, Gruffudd... put these on and let us be about our business.'

I dressed hurriedly in the proffered garments; the undyed woollen habit and cowl of a Cistercian monk, as well as a long stave, such as those used by monks and friars on long hikes.

'Ah! And let us not forget these.'

He drew a further two objects from the cupboard and handed one of them to me. It was a belt to which was attached a long, vicious looking dagger in a leather scabbard.

'Tie that to your waist beneath the habit, but in such a way as to be able to draw it swiftly if needed.' He gave me a meaningful look. He was right, of course. The dagger could make all the difference between killing or being killed if we were challenged. My mouth was suddenly dry and I swallowed awkwardly as I turned to follow him out of the stables. We walked slowly across the wide courtyard from the stables to the front gate, practising the gait of weary holy men on a long pilgrimage. It was pleasing to see that we had fooled the guard at the gate when he challenged us.

'It's alright, Eryl,' said Owain as the guard realised who it was. 'We are dressed to fool Englishmen, so if we can fool you, my faithful friend, that must be a hopeful sign. Now find and saddle a horse as quickly as you can so that you may join the Lord Tudur as he leads his men from here.'

'Thank you, my lord, and may God protect you on your journey.' Then Eryl, realising that there must be real danger if his lord was making his escape in disguise, raced over to the stables in search of a mount.

We hobbled out of the gates and made for the tree line at the top of the hill I normally descended from at the end of my morning run. We reached the wood without incident and headed south. We were still less than a mile from the lodge when we heard shouting in the distance. One or both of the English forces had reached the lodge. They would meet no resistance, of course, because Tudur had long since taken our warriors south while the servants had been told to put all the ale they could find in front of de Grey's escort in the great hall, before quietly dispersing into the surrounding countryside. The hubbub soon died down and I hoped, fervently, that they would not cause any great destruction or raze the lodge. They would certainly be enraged to find that their quarry had fooled them and made good his escape. It was easy to see how destroying Owain's home would be tempting in the circumstances. After several miles heading south we emerged from the wood into a series of low, rock strewn hills and headed east.

'Let's make our way to Valle Crucis Abbey. The monks will give us food and shelter while we work out what we do next.' Owain's face was grim. 'We will have to be very vigilant as well. We are now on open ground and if the soldiers of de Grey or Talbot see us we are certain to be challenged.'

I believe the full peril we were facing had only now fully dawned on him. The two earls would not have made such a determined effort to arrest Owain unless Bolingbroke had ordered them to do so. Now Owain was certainly outlawed as a traitor and there was no doubt that, if captured, he would be summarily tried before facing hideous execution by being hanged, drawn and quartered.

Our assumed hobbling gait slowed us considerably but we dare not move normally in case we were being observed. We were still in that rocky, treeless area when our worst fears were realised. As we approached a large outcrop of rock in which we hoped to hide and rest awhile, there was a drumming of hooves and two riders wearing the Talbot livery on their surcoats came galloping into view. We all saw each other at the same instant and they immediately turned their horses' heads and closed on us.

'Leave the talking to me and be ready for anything,' Owain murmured in a quiet but steady voice.

Then, the horsemen were upon us. The tallest in the saddle brought his mount to a halt and removed his helm, revealing a shock of ginger hair and a small, clipped beard growing reluctantly on the tip of his chin. He cut such a ridiculous figure that even in that moment of fear, I felt a strong desire to laugh. Prudently, I controlled the urge and examined the second rider. He had no helm but had dark hair and was clean-shaven. With no exchange of pleasantries the redhead regarded us with suspicion.

'Who are you and where are you from?' The voice was imperious and totally lacking in respect.

'I am Brother Gareth and my companion is Brother Gildas.' I stared at Owain in amazement, for the voice was no longer his but the tremulous, reedy tones of a very old man, the words interspersed with short rasping gasps for breath. It sounded totally authentic.

'And what of Brother Gildas, has he lost his tongue so that you must talk on his behalf?' Redhead's voice was laden with sarcasm.

Owain, however, took it in his stride and responded in a matter-of-fact manner, but again in the breathless rasp of an old man.

'Unfortunately, Brother Gildas has committed the sin of adultery, and must atone for it by keeping silent for a whole year. Have you ever committed such a sin, my friend?' Owain followed the question with an understanding smile which Redhead found most irritating, for he glared at Owain, his face flushing angrily.

'Come on, Dunstan.' His companion spoke for the first time. 'I believe we are wasting our time here. Let's go and find the real Glendower instead of losing precious time talking to these two.'

'Did you say Glendower, meaning Owain Glyndŵr, Lord of Sycharth and Glyndyfrdwy?' Owain interrupted, his voice taking on a crafty tone.

'Yes, the very same.' The dark-haired man leaned forward in the saddle. 'Would you know anything about his whereabouts, old one?'

'Would you consider giving a small donation to help with the upkeep of our abbey if I told you what I know?' asked Owain in a wheedling voice.

'By the bones of the saints, Monk, but you are trying my patience,' Dunstan snapped. 'If you value your scrawny life, you will tell us all you know of Glendower and you will do so now. Otherwise, you will not live to try your ridiculous demand for money on any other innocent travellers.'

'Was he on horseback?' the dark-haired companion enquired.

'No, he was travelling on foot, unless he had a horse well hidden in the undergrowth,' Owain said.

'You had better go and investigate, Roland,' said Dunstan grimly. 'Do not take him on single-handed, even if he is on foot. Come back for me and we will take him together. By all accounts he is an experienced and capable soldier, sure to be dangerous if cornered.'

Roland smiled, kicked his heels into his horse's flanks and cantered away in search of his quarry.

'Well now, we had better be on our way,' Owain said wearily. 'We have a long way to go.'

'Hold on, old man. Not so fast,' Dunstan chuckled. He rubbed his chin with his gauntleted hand, then frowned. 'You are both dressed like monks, though Gildas is by far the biggest monk I have ever seen. Now you, Brother Gareth, look and sound like a monk, so why is it that something about the two of you troubles me? Something does not quite fit, so before you go I intend to find out whether my little hunch is correct.'

Suddenly my mouth felt very dry and my heart began to beat a lot faster.

'Why don't you both remove your cowls so I can see

your tonsured heads? Just do it slowly, and without sudden movements.' Dunstan smiled again, though there was little mirth in his eyes as he drew his sword to enforce the command.

For a moment we both remained motionless, then in one incredibly swift but smooth movement, Owain drew his hand from the folds of his habit raising it behind his head before throwing the long dagger with deadly accuracy. Dunstan's eyes widened momentarily while he opened his mouth, presumably to call to Roland but the shout was stillborn as the metal blade scythed into his neck close to his Adam's apple before the tip emerged from the other side. Instead of a shout I heard an ugly, gurgling sound in his throat; then two fountains of blood poured out of his neck and mouth as he tried to claw at the fatally embedded blade. Then, his body collapsed slowly, like a rag doll, rolling out of the saddle to slither, lifeless, to the ground.

I stood still, severely shaken by the sudden, violent and bloody death of the soldier. I turned my back on Owain and was violently sick. Meanwhile, the battle-hardened Lord of Sycharth and Glyndyfrdwy coolly grabbed hold of the horse's reins.

'Come on, Gruffudd,' he snapped. 'I know you are not used to such violence and death, but it was either him or us. Now pull yourself together. We must both mount this horse and ride as quickly as we can from here. Let's drag this loudmouth behind a rock. We have no time to hide the corpse properly. There could be many more of his companions in the area for all we know.'

Understanding the danger, I forced movement back into my limbs and climbed onto the horse behind Owain as he urged the animal away from that fateful place. As we rode away I had plenty to occupy my mind. I found it extremely difficult to force the image of Owain, calmly removing his bloody dagger from the dead Dunstan's neck and wiping the blade clean on the man's surcoat, from my mind. And his story of how I, or rather Brother Gildas, had to undertake a vow of silence for a year for committing the sin of adultery made me wonder whether he knew about my feelings for Mared and had used that knowledge, in a moment of danger, not just to save my skin but to let me know that he was aware of my feelings for his wife. While I had never dreamt of committing adultery, indeed I had been at pains to hide my feelings even from the lady, the possibility that he knew the situation filled me with a terrible guilt. Yet, he had never wavered in the sincerity of his friendship towards me. That did not lighten my guilt either.

'You are very quiet, Gruffudd. What ails you?' Owain had to shout to make himself heard above a considerable headwind and the drumming of the horse's hooves, as we attempted to gain as much ground as possible before the horse became exhausted from galloping under our combined weight.

'Nothing, my lord,' I lied. 'I simply thought that holding a conversation would be difficult in the circumstances.'

Owain seemed to accept my explanation and we both concentrated on making the poor animal's task as easy as we possibly could by positioning and moving our bodies in concert with his. After a mile or so at the gallop our mount slowed to a canter, blowing noticeably, and Owain allowed the change in pace, realising that the horse was feeling the strain of our combined weight. He seemed better able to cope with it at a canter and he kept that up for another half-hour before showing serious signs of distress. My lord slowed him to a walk, half a mile from a small wood nestling on the southern slopes of the Berwyn mountains, which we had been approaching all the while. Once we had gained the shelter of the trees we stopped, dismounted and allowed our spent horse to rest. It was the first week in September, and the approaching evening was still laden with the balmy warmth of summer. We found some stale bread in the saddlebags, and thanks to our growing hunger pangs, it tasted much better than its appearance had suggested. Meanwhile, the stolen horse had recovered its breath and was grazing gratefully close at hand, but was in no condition to be ridden again that day. We rested there quietly for some time before Owain stood up once again.

'We must move on if we are to reach Valle Crucis Abbey before nightfall,' he said briskly. 'The horse has served us well and the least we can do is find him a stable to rest in. We will call him Lightning, in honour of his brave effort, but first we must get rid of all trace of the Talbot livery. Lightning must appear to be an ordinary horse belonging to two weary travellers, and we must rid him of all trappings of war and any connection to the Earl Talbot.'

So, I mused, I had been correct in my guess of where we were headed. The lonely Valley of the Cross close to the river Dee was named after Eliseg's Cross, a Christian memorial which had stood there for several centuries. The influential Valle Crucis Abbey had been founded in 1201 under the patronage of Madog ap Gruffudd, Prince of Powys Fadog, a direct ancestor of Glyndŵr. The stone-built abbey had been constructed on the site of an older timber-built church, within sight of Eliseg's Cross. For the next eighty years it had been the spiritual base for the whole area, just as the brooding mountain top fortress of Dinas Brân, early home of the Powys Fadog dynasty, had been its political base. Now, two centuries later, Valle Crucis was still a flourishing community of Cistercian choir monks and lay brothers. Dinas Brân, however, had long since been abandoned by the descendants of Madog ap Gruffudd, though Owain was still a popular and respected Lord of Glyndyfrdwy and he and his family continued to be held in high esteem by the monks of Valle Crucis.

The desolate castle of Dinas Brân was largely in ruins, though one of its towers was still habitable and had become the home of a female sect which still practised the old druidic religion. This fiercely independent group of women were held in awe and fear by ordinary folk, who believed they were a powerful coven of witches who knew the secret of casting the evil eye, and were best given a wide berth. A strange, secretive lot, they professed to despise men and would only allow young virgins to become noviciates of their community. Some years before, Tudur had taken me up to Dinas Brân to see the castle. As we climbed the final steep slope to the castle's tumbledown entrance I was startled by an eerie, hissing noise which I had never experienced before. Tudur noticed my nervousness and laughed.

'Not to worry, axeman, they are just a group of women, mostly of a venerable age, who are warning us to keep our distance. The noise is made by dozens of wooden rattles to which are attached the skulls of small animals, rodents mostly, which they shake vigorously. They obviously have not recognised me yet or they would stop making the infernal din.'

'How do they know you?' I could not hide the surprise in my voice. 'Everyone knows that these weird women hate all men.'

'Almost all men,' Tudur grinned mysteriously. 'We are nearly there, Gruffudd. You will see that they treat me with respect. I have no idea how they will react to you, though.' He paused, then laughed again at my unease. 'But worry not, they will not cast the evil eye upon you while you are with me.' Tudur obviously found the situation amusing. I was certainly not amused but kept close to him as we entered the old ruin.

I stared aghast at a group of some two dozen women, mostly with long, tangled hair and dressed in various combinations of well-worn garments and animal skins. There were several toothless old hags and a sprinkling of young maidens, but most were, or appeared to be, middle-aged.

'When they finally vacated the old castle my great-grandfather agreed to allow this cult to shelter in the north tower, which was the only remaining section of the ancient fortress not in need of major repair. He even had the roof of the adjoining kitchens renewed so that the women could have the use of those, also. Over time they became known as Daughters of the Moon Goddess. At any rate, they never forgot the old man's kindness and ever since, they have treated the men in our family with respect. The tower was certainly an improvement on the caves they had lived in previously.'

While Tudur was explaining the situation to me the women had recognised him and stopped shaking their devilish rattles. Their leader, a tall but stooping matron in her middle years raised her arm to stop the excited chatter of her flock and limped slowly towards us. Her joints were obviously badly affected by life in the cold, wet and windy ruins of Dinas Brân.

'*Henffych*, Tudur, son of the house of Powys Fadog,' the ungainly woman croaked, her mouth splitting into a broad grin to display a few rotten teeth in scattered isolation, adorning an otherwise toothless mouth.

'And a good day to you, Earth Mother, and to all your sisters,' Tudur responded with a smile.

'I have simply come here to show my friend the old family stronghold. We will not be bothering you for long, I promise.'

'Visits from you and your brothers are no bother to us. We welcome the descendants of the noble prince who treated our cult with such kindness, all those years ago.' She paused, then frowned and glared at me. 'I do not recognise this stranger and he is not of your kin. However, we will treat him kindly... whilst he is under your protection.' She paused, pointedly, before delivering the last phrase then glared again, her pupils cold as ice. Despite my best effort at studied indifference, I could not stop the involuntary shiver which coursed down my spine. I silently cursed myself for my lack of control as a fleeting, but knowing, grin passed between the Earth Mother and Tudur. Even now the memory of that moment was unsettling.

It was dark when Owain and I reached the imposing entrance to Valle Crucis Abbey. Several lay brothers came to answer our knocking and one of the great oak doors was pulled slowly open to reveal concerned faces anxious to see who the visitors, arriving so late at night, might be. When they saw Owain the welcome was warm. While one of the lay brothers took Lightning away for a deserved meal and rest in the stables, the others led us to the refectory and plied us with bowls of *cawl* made from mutton and vegetables, the ingredients all fresh produce from the abbey's sheep flocks and gardens, washed down with splendid ale from the abbey brewery.

Some of the choir monks joined us and informed us that the Abbot had already gone to bed, though they would willingly call him if Owain wished to speak with him.

'No, there is no need to disturb the Reverend Father,' he informed them. 'Gruffudd and I are very tired, and we would like nothing better than to retire to our beds.'

We were given two monks' cells reserved for visitors with firm but comfortable beds, and despite wondering whether I would have nightmares about the killing of Talbot's retainer, I fell asleep almost immediately and enjoyed a peaceful night's slumber.

We made an early start the following morning, anxious to get back to Sycharth. The previous day's events would have serious repercussions and we both knew that however we reacted to the dangerous new situation, momentous decisions would need to be taken, and taken swiftly. Owain borrowed one of the abbey's farm horses while I rode a refreshed Lightning. We trotted down the path we had navigated in the dark the previous evening, past Eliseg's Cross. From here we would follow the track leading out of the valley and the last steep climb over the Berwyn mountains before following the broader, more fertile terrain leading towards Sycharth. As we came around a bend we saw a cowled figure walking down the path towards us. It was Aled Ddoeth, Aled the Wise, the Abbot of Valle Crucis. We reined in the horses and Owain greeted him.

'Good morning. You are up betimes, Master Abbot,' Owain addressed him with a smile.

'Nay, sire,' the Abbot said, returning his smile. 'It is you who have risen too soon – too soon by a hundred years!'

After thanking the old man for his abbey's hospitality the previous night, we were soon on our way once more. We both commented on his enigmatic words to Owain but they made little sense to either of us. However, there were so many pressing matters to discuss that we soon forgot about the Abbot's remark and, to my knowledge, Owain never mentioned the incident again.

When we reached Sycharth we had a rousing welcome, for large numbers of Owain's friends and supporters had gathered to attend a meeting he had already organised, several weeks before.

There were many familiar faces and many I had never seen before. I soon realised that this was a large gathering of the foremost of the *uchelwyr*, from all parts of Wales. In fact it was probably the largest single gathering of such people for more than a century. Even Sycharth was not big enough to house them all and many had been billeted in outhouses, temporarily converted for human habitation, while others had brought makeshift shelters which were erected in the orchard and surrounding meadows.

There was also much relief when we arrived, for Owain had arranged for the meeting to take place in the great hall at the hour of ten, and we were nearly two hours late. In addition, the guests had been informed by the worried household of the attempt by two Marcher Lords to capture Owain in Glyndyfrdwy the previous day, and no one knew whether he had escaped from the trap or been captured. Tudur and his company had all returned without encountering the enemy but Tudur had been subjected to a scathing rebuke from a distraught Mared for having left

Owain and me to make our own escape, though she knew that Tudur and his men had been ordered to do so as decoys. Tudur had done his best to comfort her, knowing it to be a frantic and alarmed reaction to the extreme danger facing her husband, and the worrying lack of news.

As soon as we had dismounted Owain ordered his lieutenants to spread the word that the assembly would take place in the great hall in half an hour, then briskly ordered me to join him for a drink and a hurried breakfast in his quarters. Mared ran to meet us and threw her arms around Owain, smothering him with kisses, all the while chiding him for having given her such a fright. Then she turned to me and kissed me on both cheeks, relieved and happy that we had both overcome great danger and were, at last, safely home.

9

HYWEL AP GRONW gave three sharp raps on the top table with his gavel. The unusually high level of noise in the overcrowded great hall gradually subsided. All seats were taken and there was a standing audience, three rows deep along all four walls of the large chamber. I had never seen so many people congregated under one roof before. By contrast only Hywel and Lord Owain were seated at the long top table.

Hywel cleared his throat a little self-consciously, then began in a strong, clear voice.

'My lords, I have been asked by Owain ap Gruffudd Fychan, Baron of Glyndyfrdwy and Lord of Cynllaith, to chair this meeting, which he has called to discuss the urgent and real dangers facing people all over Wales. As you know, the English King and his Parliament are becoming increasingly hostile. The usurper Henry Bolingbroke has imprisoned the rightful English King, Richard II, in Pontefract Castle and we know not if he is alive or dead. Many powerful men in England do not accept Henry's claim to the throne and are waiting for any opportunity to overthrow him. Henry desperately needs the support of Parliament and will do anything asked of him by its members – such as ratifying the ridiculous new penal laws. We all know that he has murdered several of the Marcher Lords, and replaced them with men who know nothing of the ancient and hard-fought-for agreements we had with their predecessors. These agreements ensured relative peace, and some respect, for Welsh nobles from English nobility in the March. The new Marcher Lords have no such regard for us and are constantly searching for excuses to confiscate our lands and to end our agreed responsibilities and standing in the area. I need not remind you of the tremendous burden of taxes placed upon us, and the poverty stricken population, by both King and Marcher Lords.' Hywel ap Gronw paused for a moment, allowing the glum atmosphere his words had created to harden.

'Now, that is a brief summation of the position we are in, as people of Wales. It leaves us in a very precarious and exposed position. We have two stark choices. We can accept that we are a conquered race and watch the English deprive us of all our rights through their vicious new penal laws. That is the road to slavery, dishonour and the gradual but irrevocable extinction of the Welsh people, our customs, our literature, our history and language. Alternatively, we can take up arms against our oppressors, as many of our illustrious ancestors have done over the centuries, and win back our rights, our lands and secure our future as a people, by force of arms.'

The second option was greeted with shouts of approval and much stamping of feet on the stone floor. Hywel raised his hand for silence before continuing.

'Of course, the success of taking the second option is by no means guaranteed. You must remember that we would be taking on one of the leading powers in Europe. The English can put at least twelve soldiers into the field to each one of ours. They are far wealthier than we are and their much larger armies will be better armed, better equipped, better paid and, probably, better fed. So you see, whichever option we choose, the omens are far from good.'

The hall erupted once more, but this time there was anger and frustration in the shouting, with many arguing amongst themselves. Hywel used his gavel to bang the table once more, and gradually the hubbub subsided.

'My lords, friends, you did not come here today just to listen. I realise that many of you will want an opportunity to express your own views. I now intend to ask for speakers and, afterwards, when those who wish to speak have had their say, my Lord Owain will address you.'

A tall, middle-aged, acerbic looking man in the front row of seats was the first to speak. He spoke with a strong southern accent.

'I am Baron Henry Dwn of Cydweli (Kidwelly). Of one thing I am certain. There is only one honourable course we can take, and that is to take up arms against Bolingbroke. We must do so quickly, before he finds some excuse to come and murder us in our beds. However, there is another matter to be decided upon even more urgently. We must have a decisive and powerful leader. I believe we have such a person in this room but I will allow others, who know him much better than I do, to name him.'

Henry Dwn was looking directly at Owain as he spoke.

'We have heard of how the English are much more powerful than we are. When united and unchallenged, that is correct. But, at present, Henry IV is at his weakest. Internally he has many enemies who would be happy to slit his throat, so he has to be continually on his guard. He cannot do anything without carrying Parliament with him and the royal coffers are, by all accounts, pretty empty. In addition, the French, the Scots, and the Irish are presenting him with a variety of military problems. What I am trying to say, gentlemen, is this; with Henry preoccupied with so many problems both within his realm and with other nations, there will never be a better time to start a revolt against English rule than now.'

The south Walian sat down to resounding applause, for his reasoning had been both perceptive and appropriate, and many in the hall were heartened by his optimistic attitude. However, another man had jumped to his feet. Many in the hall knew him and most of them disliked him. He now waited impatiently for the noise to dissipate.

'I am Baron Hywel Selyf of Nannau, near Dolgellau, and a cousin of Owain Glyndŵr. Talk is cheap. Talk of an armed insurrection against King Henry IV is a nonsense and, let us be clear, an act of treason, punishable by execution by means of hanging, drawing and quartering. Is there anyone in this hall who would relish the prospect of being executed in such a manner?' He was interrupted by murmurs of disagreement which quickly became loud and angry protests so that Hywel Selyf's voice was drowned.

Hywel ap Gronw rose quickly and used his gavel again to restore order. 'My lords, gentlemen please... We are forgetting ourselves. This is a formal meeting requesting views. Every speaker has a right to express his views and opinions. You may disagree, but the speaker is not to be interrupted while he is presenting his views. If you wish to take issue with those views you must wait to be called upon to speak. My Lord Nannau, please continue.'

'Thank you, chairman. I do not believe in this idea that we only have two options open to us, for there is clearly a third. That is to unite in reaffirming our allegiance to the English throne, making it clear to Henry and to all English people that we seek peaceful co-existence with them and that we wish to be loyal subjects of the English crown. I'm afraid that our days as the *Cymry*, with our own language, customs and laws, are over. We must accept the reality that we have a larger, more powerful neighbour who will be much better inclined towards us as a friend. When we have proved this, after a few years, by carrying out our promise, the chances are that the vicious penal laws we now endure will be revoked. Only then will we be accepted as equals by the English, but we will have ensured a bright future for our children and the generations to come.'

Hywel Selyf sat down to howls of derision and threats from the incensed majority. Then, a hunchback stood up somewhere in the rear seating area. He was short and powerfully built, but with a large hump just behind his left shoulder which forced him to hold his head in an awkward, right-leaning position. He was, however, dressed in expensive clothes and was clearly a man of means.

'I am Dafydd ap Llywelyn ap Hywel Fychan, better known, perhaps, as Dafydd Gam, Lord of Brycheiniog, and direct descendant of the kings of the ancient kingdom of Brycheiniog.'

The man responded to the gasps of surprise and several uncomplimentary comments which greeted his announcement, with a malevolent smile directed at Lord Owain.

'I do not expect my views to carry much weight in this place, so I will not keep you long. However, I feel it is my duty to warn you of the chaos you are about to create and the painful and crushing defeat you will surely endure. You are doomed to visit untold misery upon the Welsh people which will last for generations, and all in pursuit of a foolish, impossible dream. With the exception of the noble and sensible Hywel Selyf, what I have heard so far this day is ill-conceived, dangerous nonsense. It is time you examined the current situation with your heads, not with nostalgic wallowing in our history and sentimental tales of bygone heroes. Those heroes would have been just as powerless as we are today against the might of England.'

At this point Dafydd Gam's voice was lost as tempers boiled over and several individuals rushed forward to grab hold of him.

'Hold!' The authoritative voice from the top table stopped Gam's attackers in their tracks and silenced all the others. Owain Glyndŵr was standing in an angry posture, his eyes blazing with anger.

'What are we – a band of nobles or a savage rabble? Whatever you may think of Dafydd Gam's words, he has come here to contribute to a discussion which may well lead to decisions of great import to the Welsh nation. Dafydd has the same right to be heard as anyone else. You will have the opportunity to make your own views known later. Meanwhile, anyone who attempts to lay hands upon or harry a speaker again will be thrown out of this hall.'

'I thank you, my lord, for saving my unworthy skin from the mob,' Dafydd Gam responded with mock gravity. 'There you are, my beauties,' he continued, his voice loaded with sarcasm. 'There is your saviour – the great leader, *Y Mab Darogan*, the Son of Prophecy, who is destined to lead you to victory over King Henry IV of England. It is also true that by ignoring the muster for the King's campaign in Scotland, he will almost certainly be declared an outlaw and have his lands forfeited on His Majesty's impending return. So now he calls this meeting in desperation, hoping that you will all be foolish enough to proclaim him your *Tywysog*, and join in a grand rebellion against the English.'

There was pandemonium once more as the hunchback sat down with a satisfied grin. However, there were no more attempts to manhandle him.

It took Hywel ap Gronw several minutes to silence the furious majority following Dafydd Gam's parting shots, so blatantly calculated to insult Owain Glyndŵr.

The next speaker was Rhys ap Tudur, bristling with indignation at Dafydd Gam's personal attack on Owain, and angrily rejecting the notion expressed by both the previous two speakers that challenging the English was a foolish idea, doomed to failure. He went on to ridicule the belief that the Welsh were finished as a nation and that accepting English rule, values and language was the only way forward. His every sentence was cheered to the rafters.

'I will leave you with one thought. I do not know whether there is a *Mab Darogan*. May those of you who believe that Owain is *Y Mab Darogan*, please continue to believe so. The rest of you, like me, know that Owain Glyndŵr is the last genuine claimant to the hereditary title, *Tywysog Cymru* or Prince of Wales. I also believe that his abilities as a warrior, as a war leader, and as a highly educated and refined scholar, qualify him as our supreme leader in any case. He has impressed friend and foe as a man of honour and integrity who has shown through insight and wisdom that he has a firm grasp of the principles of statesmanship. It is sufficient to know that he has all the qualities required to lead us to freedom. Now what about you? Are you mice? Or are you men – real men – real *Cymry*? That is the question you must ask yourselves this day. I think you all know where I stand on this matter.'

He sat down abruptly to shouts of approval and acclaim. Rhys Tudur was one of the famous Tudors of Penmynydd and a former Sheriff of Anglesey, whose foster mother was sister to Owain's mother. He was, himself, a respected leader and an accomplished warrior. Now, he had thrown his weight solidly behind Glyndŵr, adding even more to the powerful, supportive tide of feeling in the hall.

Another six of the *uchelwyr* spoke, each enthusiastically supporting the proclamation of Owain as *Tywysog Cymru* and endorsing a call to arms.

Hywel ap Gronw rose once more, but there was no need for a gavel for a great hush fell over the great hall as Owain, also, got to his feet. An introduction was not required, so Hywel simply bowed to his lord and resumed his seat in silence.

Owain stood, feet apart, head held high, the golden mane framing the bearded face and distinctive eyes. Despite having reached his middle years he looked every inch the noble prince, the powerful war leader. His whole being radiated a distinctive magnetism so that we all waited, holding our breath, conscious that we were in the presence of someone with that elusive, yet influential quality, which defines great men and sets them apart from ordinary mortals.

'My lords, fellow Welshmen, friends – in my view today's meeting has been an interesting and positive one for, even before I call a vote, it is pretty evident where the majority lies. It has been a fair and frank discussion, ably chaired by Hywel ap Gronw and, in the main, the discussion has concentrated on policies and strategies rather than on personal attacks on individuals. For that I thank you. However, before we vote on these fateful matters, I would like to say a few simple words to close the forum. Firstly, I would remind you that we, the *Cymry*, are the descendants of a noble race that once controlled the whole of what is now England and Wales. Contrary to the beliefs of our enemies, we were, and are, a civilised people who were greatly influenced by the language and culture of the Romans who conquered large tracts of Britain from our British ancestors. The Romans brought with them a civilisation drawn not only from their own history and culture but from the cultures of many other civilisations, not least being that of the Greeks. We, the evolving Welsh nation, learned to control our country in an orderly, civilised manner and, significantly, we embraced Christianity several centuries before the invading Vikings and Anglo-Saxons, following the departure of the Roman legions. We were eventually driven from our homes in the rich lands of what is now England into the mountains, hills and marshes of Wales. But we kept our language and culture, our methods of governance and the just laws of Hywel Dda. It was only in 1282, with the underhanded killing of Llywelyn ap Gruffudd, the last to take the title Prince of Wales, that we had to bow the knee to Edward I. Even he, merciless King that he was, realised it was in his interests to allow the Welsh *uchelwyr* to control the Welsh populace in his name. But successive English kings have gradually allowed Parliament and certain Marcher Lords to tighten their direct control over Wales in the belief that we are a conquered and broken race, powerless to resist.'

Here Owain paused, allowing the full meaning of his assessment of current English thinking to sink in, the piercing feline eyes turning keenly to every corner of the hall. He waited, knowing that he held everyone, even his critics, in the palm of his hand. Then, in a quiet, almost casual tone, he continued.

'Have we as *uchelwyr* really been reduced to a rabble, because that is what the London Parliament thinks we are? Only a few months ago when I went to London to reclaim land stolen from me by Reginald de Grey, they refused me saying – and these were their words – "What care we for barefoot Welsh rascals"... Are we really prepared to allow followers of Bolingbroke, the usurper, to talk of us in that vein and go meekly about our business? For that is what Dafydd Gam and my cousin, Hywel Selyf want us to do? Do we still have our pride? Do we still have the courage of our ancestors? Do we have the will to show the world that we are a nation with a distinct identity – a nation of noble lineage which is not prepared to be simply one additional English province?'

As he spoke his voice gradually rose in volume to a shout. The hall was an instant cauldron of noise as those on their feet bellowed their defiance, while many of the seated jumped to their feet knocking over tables and chairs in the rush to add their voices to the general pandemonium. The shouting went on for some minutes and Owain raised a hand and signalled one of his stewards to open the main doors, for he had seen Dafydd Gam and Hywel Selyf sidling cautiously with their few retainers towards the great doors, obviously fearing for their lives. The worked-up majority were still making too much noise to notice the sounds of the door bolts being released or the creaking of the iron hinges as the dissenters raced out into the September sunshine, more concerned with saving their lives than making a dignified exit. The doors were closed again and Owain raised both hands for silence.

'Well, my friends, that was a ringing endorsement if ever I heard one. Now that the few speakers against rebellion have left the hall I do not think we need to take a vote on the matter. However, just in case there are other objectors present, may I ask anyone who disagrees with the idea of rebelling against English rule to kindly raise their hands?'

Owain grinned as some wag at the back of the hall shouted, 'Nobody is going to be that foolish, my lord.'

'It has been clear to me for some years now that we would be forced into open rebellion during the next ten years or so. The unexpected and unlawful enthronement of Henry Bolingbroke has changed the situation dramatically, and as most speakers have observed we now have our backs to the wall, having been stripped of all our rights and privileges. My friends, we are not only a conquered race, but an enslaved one with no future and no hope. However, we do have the choice of standing up for ourselves and showing the English that we are still determined enough, and proud enough, to take on overwhelming odds in our struggle for the right to live as a free society. It will be a state where equality before the law, our law, will be the norm for all, and where fair play will have an unalienable, central role.'

Owain paused briefly for a round of applause to die away.

'I thank you for today's resounding endorsement of that view and I welcome the great privilege you have bestowed upon me by asking me to lead you. There is no time to lose and I invite you all and any others of like mind to be present at my home in Glyndyfrdwy in two days' time for my proclamation as *Tywysog Cymru*, and the formal declaration of war against Henry IV of England. Thank you for taking part in this assembly. I now look forward to meeting you all again at Glyndyfrdwy on the sixteenth of September, in two days from now.'

As the excited throng left the hall I moved forward towards the top table where Owain and Hywel ap Gronw now sat in earnest conversation. Hywel looked animated and eager but Owain appeared contemplative, as if adjusting to the turn of events which had suddenly thrust him into the leadership of a small nation preparing for war against a mighty neighbour. I could imagine how the sudden realisation of many heavy responsibilities would weigh upon such a man. He and his family would also have to adjust to giving up positions of authority and social standing within the tightly-knit Marcher lordships, as well as the nominal acceptance of King and Parliament. Indeed, his proposed declaration as Prince of Wales would be a direct challenge to the young Prince Henry, who had already been declared Prince of Wales by his father, Bolingbroke. Following the tradition instigated by Edward I, Owain, his family and followers would all be declared outlaws the moment the news reached the King's ears. His days as a rich landowner with two homes and a position of acceptance within the English hierarchy would be over for ever.

I stepped up to the top table platform and was suddenly jostled by someone eager to push past me. I reached out instinctively and grabbed a scrawny arm to check and turn the cheeky rascal. It was the detestable Crach Ffinnant, who began to struggle angrily but ineffectually in my grip.

'Let go of me, you big lump – can you not see that I am anxious to talk to our Prince?'

'Of course I will, Great Prophet, once you have apologised for trying to shove me out of your way. You see, I too am on course to speak to our lord, and I was ahead of you.'

As I spoke I started to squeeze a pressure point just above

his elbow and further angry words were strangled in a squeal of pain as I increased the pressure a little.

'Will you stop your infernal squabbling,' Hywel called irritably. 'Owain has weighty matters to consider and you two are not helping him with this childish confrontation.'

I switched my gaze to Owain who was looking at me with a surprisingly indulgent smile. 'Let go of Crach, Gruffudd. I will speak with him first, but I intend having a serious discussion with Lady Mared at supper this evening and I would like you to be present. So you will have as much time as you wish to discuss anything and everything with me then over a quiet, private meal and a tankard or two of fine Shrewsbury ale.'

On hearing that Owain would speak to him first, Crach afforded me a superior smile which soon collapsed into a jealous scowl as he learned of our leader's arrangements for the evening. When he reached Owain's side, however, his face had taken on its usual fawning, obsequious smile as he sought to impress and to please. I slipped away in disgust, and went to my quarters for a wash and a change of clothing. I always wanted to look and feel my best in the company of the lovely Lady Mared.

When I finally knocked and entered the Glyndŵr private quarters I was surprised to find Owain in an unusually sombre mood. Mared seemed cheerful enough and she came over to welcome me immediately with her usual kiss on both my cheeks, a feature which, despite all my years in their service, still made me blush furiously. Owain usually found this most amusing. Tonight, however, he did not seem to notice, motioning me quietly to my seat at table, opposite the two of them.

He hardly said a word during the meal other than to voice his appreciation of the delicious roast pork. My lady kept drawing me into generalities about the autumnal weather now that mid-September had settled into a pattern of cold winds and rain, warning us that the winter frosts would soon be upon us. All the while she cast anxious glances at Owain, though she made no attempt to break his self-imposed silence. We both knew that he was struggling to come to terms with some difficult issues and eventually he would share some of his concerns with us.

I was the last to finish eating. I am a big man with an appetite to match, and Owain would oftentimes make some amusing remark about my capacity for eating, but he seemed impervious to eating habits for the moment.

'Would you gentlemen wish me to return to my ladies so that you can speak in private?' Mared inquired archly, giving me a look.

'On the contrary,' Owain responded quickly. 'I would like you to stay for I have important matters that need to be aired which will affect all three of us.' With this he stood up and recharged his own tankard and mine with ale. 'Would you like some small beer, my love, or a glass of wine perhaps? No? Ah well, let us sit around the fire where it will be more comfortable.'

The first log fire for months was crackling crisply in the large fireplace, the fresh yellow flames spiralling invitingly up the chimney, as welcoming as an old friend. Mared and Owain sat together on the settle to one side of the hearth while I leaned back, replete, in the armchair opposite. Owain, with some deliberation, placed his tankard down on the bare, flagstoned floor, turned towards Mared and took one of her slim hands in both his own.

'You and I have been man and wife for many years, my dear. During those years we have had some wonderful times together. We have raised a large brood of children, we have had periods of enforced absences when I had to go away to fight for an English King, but in the main we have had a comfortable life here at Sycharth and at Glyndyfrdwy, surrounded by friends and loyal tenants and servants, wanting for nothing. I had hoped to maintain this lifestyle for the rest of our days. Unfortunately, Henry Bolingbroke has put an end to that and I am now faced with the most difficult decision of my life. Indeed, it could be argued that the decision has been made for me, for my people and others in many parts of Wales are asking me to realise a prophecy, a dream which we, the *Cymry*, have believed in for many centuries. They believe that in these dangerous times I must give life to the prophecy of *Y Mab Darogan* and free our land from the English yoke.'

He stared keenly at Mared, searching for some reaction. To his surprise, and mine, she smiled gently at him, placing her free hand over both of his. It was a sad little smile and there was a hint of tears in the lovely eyes. She cleared her throat but her voice was still husky when she spoke.

'I know, my lord. I realise we have only touched on this over the past weeks and months, and I'm well aware that you have done your very best to shield me and the girls from the frightening reality of what lies ahead. I also understand your position, and that there is no honourable way you can refuse to agree to their wishes. Indeed, to be proclaimed *Tywysog Cymru* is the highest honour a Welshman can be given and English kings do not have the right to claim that title for their eldest sons. The first requirement is that he must be of Welsh royal blood.'

She stopped abruptly, as if she thought she had said too much. For a moment or two there was silence as Owain and I stared at her in amazement. Her little speech had shown us that she had been following the political twists and turns with a keen interest over many months at least. It also showed that she had a clear understanding of some of the key issues. Women did not usually take too much interest in political matters and it was rare for a man to hear a woman expressing a viewpoint on such things. But why should ladies not have their own views and opinions? I had always believed Mared to be blessed with intelligence and wisdom, and we should not have been surprised at her perspicacity. I wondered how many more ladies throughout the land possessed such knowledge and understanding of matters which had always been regarded as the preserve of men? Would there ever be a time when women's views would carry the same weight as those of their menfolk? I cannot see that happening in our present society, but the world might well be a very different place in some distant future.

'I had no idea you were following events so closely, Mared. My belief that I was keeping you shielded from worrying tidings was obviously misplaced. I still need to know whether you understand why we now need to move swiftly and whether you fully realise the precarious life we will face, at least until I can get Welshmen everywhere to flock to my banner.'

My lord's face was lined with anxiety as he gazed earnestly at his wife.

'Then let me reassure you, my Golden One, that I do. Everyone knows that Lord Grey of Ruthin is one of the King's favourites and is using that fact to try and steal your land piecemeal, with the connivance of Henry and

Parliament. They are also aware that Grey deliberately held back the King's command to muster for service in Scotland until it was too late for you to obey or indeed to inform Henry that you could not join him. This is certain to make the usurper declare you and all your family outlaws and traitors, so we will lose our homes and lands in any case, and you, and maybe others of our family, will be executed. I foresee that for this winter, you will not be strong enough to wage all-out war because, as in any rebellion, it will take time to gather impetus. No, we will have to go into hiding, and you and I may well have to part and forsake each other's company for weeks, or even months, this winter.'

For a while there was silence. Owain and I stared at Mared with undisguised admiration. Here was a woman who, without seeking advice from any man, had made it her business to know how the troubles were mounting for her husband and his followers, and had thought through the possible grievous consequences that could engulf him and the family.

'I hope I have not displeased you by behaving in such an unladylike manner,' she murmured, at length.

'Displeased – me?' Owain turned to me smiling proudly. 'Did you hear that, Gruffudd?' Then he turned back and gathered her in his arms. 'My love, at this moment I am the proudest husband in all of Wales. You have shown resourcefulness and concern for me and our family, in equal measure. It must have been a lonely task for you – piecing together the facts and weighing their significance as they occurred with nobody to share your worries. You have been incredibly brave and I salute you as a most amazing, courageous person. From now on we will discuss not only personal and family matters as we have always done, but affairs of state as well. I suspect you could yet be my most trusted and perceptive advisor. What say you, Gruffudd?'

'Well said, my lord. As you know, I have been a great admirer of my lady's talents and courage ever since we first met. I have always known that she is perceptive and shrewd with a strong interest in the arts, particularly poetry. It has been an honour and a privilege for me to compose the occasional *cywydd* in her honour. I have to confess, I was not aware of her keen interest in politics, but, as with everything else she turns her mind to, if it is her will to study politics I feel sure that her advice will be based on thorough knowledge of the subject and...'

I had to force myself to stop for I could have extolled Mared's virtues for a great deal longer, and betrayed my deep feelings for her in the process. I felt very self-conscious for a moment for she was smiling at me warmly, her eyes sparkling. Owain, too, was looking at me with a shrewd half-smile, which made me feel guilty and uncomfortable.

It was Mared who broke the silence.

'Thank you, Gruffudd. You have said some very nice things but I doubt I could live up to them.'

'I happen to agree with him,' Owain said briskly. 'You are certainly much more than a pretty face, my dear, and it is time I woke up to that fact. You could be very useful to me as a second pair of eyes and ears, and a most reliable sounding board on all sorts of issues. And you, Master Bard, can start working on another *cywydd* of praise to your lady, but preferably with little or no reference to tonight's discussion. I mean, the fewer around me who know that Mared is a student of politics and affairs of state, the freer will their conversation be and we might pick up important news and information which, otherwise, we would not be aware of.

Much of it would probably be tittle-tattle, of course. On the other hand, it might be news of threats, or the need for urgent action, which could help save our lives.'

His assumption was correct and I was reminded, yet again, that I was dealing with a man with a razor-sharp mind who never missed an opportunity to make the most of his assets, even if the asset happened to be his wife.

Owain suddenly seemed rejuvenated and anxious to begin the task of uniting his countrymen behind him in the coming, fateful war, which would settle both his future and that of the Welsh nation. Mared had not only made it her business to learn all about the high politics which had led to the current situation, but was both capable of, and willing to stand at his side to help plan proactive actions, and suitable reactions, to his enemies' efforts to destroy him. This was a revelation which seemed to have galvanised him with a new enthusiasm and self-belief, which I found quite infectious.

My lady made her excuses soon after and retired to her bed. Owain and I talked, planned, and drank some more of the fine Shrewsbury ale. When at last we decided it was time to catch up on some sleep, for the next days and weeks were sure to be long and stressful ones, he turned to me and said thoughtfully, 'Well, old friend, what will be will be, and we can only hope that fate, or the old gods, will be on our side and will see fit to help us. Meanwhile, we would be wise to do everything we can in practical terms to prepare and plan for our cause's success. It is not the best time to start hostilities with winter just around the corner, but we have neither the time nor the means to control that. In practical terms, finding a safe refuge to hide for the hard winter months will be a challenge. Indeed, I may well have to seek shelter somewhere in the mountains. Should that be so, I will have to find a more comfortable, yet safe, haven for Mared and the younger children. It follows that I will want you, Gruffudd of the Battleaxe, to go with her as her personal protector, a duty you have performed willingly and with distinction so often in the past. Will you agree to do that old friend? Bear in mind that the dangers will now be significantly greater.'

Seeing the complete trust and sincerity shining in the handsome golden eyes I knelt before him and said quietly, 'My Lord Owain, I have long been your devoted servant and, though I do not share your exalted lineage, I also dare to regard myself as one of your friends. Tonight, you are still my lord; in two days from now you will be my prince and your wishes will still be my command, an honour and a privilege which I will willingly carry out. Looking after the Princess of Wales will be a pleasure, whatever the dangers involved. Anyone seeking to harm her will have to answer to me and I swear to you, as God is my witness, I will lay down my life before she is allowed to come to any harm.' I stood up but with my head still bowed. Owain grasped my arms in a strong grip.

'Look up, my good and loyal friend. You do not have to bow your head to me. You have long earned the right to stand before me and look me straight in the eye. I, too, regard you as a friend and I am honoured to do so. If only I had thirty thousand men such as you…' He cleared his throat, turned away abruptly, and left the room without another word.

10

I T WAS AN unusually warm, pleasant June morning in 1401 on the small flat plateau which forms the summit of Mynydd Hyddgen. I sat with my back to a west-facing crag, for the strong sunshine had forced me to seek some shade. The glorious blue sky was devoid of even a wisp of cloud and the only sign of life was the presence of a majestic golden eagle gliding lazily around the acres of blue, its seven-foot wingspan reduced to insignificance by the height from which it surveyed the treeless monotony of the mid Wales highlands, crowned by the predominantly grassy slopes of Pumlumon below.

For a moment my attention was drawn to a scrabbling among some loose shale close by. A rabbit suddenly appeared. It stared at me, startled. Then, satisfied that I did not pose an immediate threat, it stood on its hind legs sniffing the air, instinctively aware of danger, but unable to pinpoint its nature. I glanced skywards and realised that the eagle was plunging to earth at breakneck speed, its great wings furled as it plummeted. For an instant I experienced a cold fear as I wondered if I was its target. Suddenly, the rabbit squealed in alarm as a long shadow briefly blotted out the sky, and ran for its life. The great raptor spread its huge wings, using superb skill to control the dive before levelling out just feet off the ground. Instead of pouncing on its target, as a hawk would have done, the eagle took up station directly behind its prey and, as the desperate rabbit ran for a bolt-hole still screaming in alarm, it glided expertly in pursuit, travelling at three times the speed of its victim. Then, it lowered its legs, the vicious talons curved and spread for maximum effect and the poor creature was whipped up into the air, still giving heart-rending voice to its pain and terror. The golden eagle gave one harsh squeal of triumph and, with its powerful wings flapping with deceptive slowness, gained height rapidly, heading north to its Snowdonia home, taking its hapless prey to an inevitable fate.

For a moment I sat there, stunned by the sheer speed and skill of the chase. I could not help feeling distress at the cruel finality of the poor rabbit's plight, yet my distress was mixed with admiration for the golden eagle's incredibly fast perception of a feeding opportunity from such a height, and the clinical skill of its actions in capturing its prey. It was a classic example of nature at work. Qualities such as human compassion did not enter into the equation. It was simply a living creature preserving its existence at the expense of another living creature. It represented the natural order of things. The rabbit's hysterical fear, pain and, no doubt, cruel death was not a consideration. In simple terms, it was the survival of the fittest. I found all this very difficult to square with Christian principles of charity, consideration for our fellow man and other living creatures. What would a priest have to say about the rights of the rabbit, I wondered? Patently, it did not have any, according to the rules of nature. There seemed to me to be strong parallels between the rules of nature and those of politics. In the end – might was right; witness the overthrow of Richard II by Bolingbroke. No doubt Owain Glyndŵr's struggle for Welsh independence would be decided eventually in victory for might, which would not necessarily have any bearing on right, or justice or fairness, but purely on the subjugation of one group of people by another, stronger group.

I had arrived in the Hyddgen Valley in the wilderness of the Pumlumon highlands three weeks earlier, with the bulk of Owain's forces. Summer in these parts was not much fun, with days of dampness and mist interspersed with others of steady rain, ranging from drizzle to outright deluge. An advance force had reached the area several weeks prior to our arrival to prepare a semi-permanent camp, which would act as a base for daring raids on both mid and west Wales, areas which, until now, had been untouched by the burgeoning rebellion. In the weeks following the arrival of Owain's total force of around five hundred men, he had led two raiding parties, each numbering a hundred and fifty men, to attack English settlements. The first attack had been on the county town of Montgomery which was taken by surprise and sacked. They then attacked Welshpool, parts of which were set on fire.

On his return to Siambr Trawsfynydd, his well-hidden base to the north-east of the Hyddgen Valley, Owain chose another one hundred and fifty men to harry English and Flemish settlements and holdings in south Cardiganshire and Pembrokeshire. This time I was chosen for my first-ever taste of real warfare, albeit in the form of surprise attacks, using hit-and-run tactics. It was very different from what I had expected, despite my years of training with the battleaxe. The rush of adrenaline mixed with nervous tension preceding every attack; the excitement of facing an enemy in a fight for your life; chasing startled, desperate men fleeing from a brutal death. And yes, then the deflation of the aftermath when you lay down on a blanket in some dark, silent glade filled with the inevitable remorse and shame as you tried to forget some of your deeds that day and the numbing realisation that you had lost some of your own humanity and self-respect during the horrors of the actual event – not at all the glory of victory that the storytellers and we, the bards, are so quick to praise. Of course, a few days later, we were greeted back in camp as heroes, not least because we were driving large numbers of stolen sheep and cattle before us, ensuring that everyone would have a plentiful supply of milk, beef, mutton and wool for a considerable time to come.

However, Owain wanted to keep up the pressure on west Wales to make Henry IV realise that we had embarked on an all-out war throughout our country, and that this was not some minor, ineffectual rebellion confined to the north. On his return to camp he instructed his brother, Tudur, to select a fresh band of a hundred and fifty men to carry the raids right down to the south of Pembrokeshire, broadening the area of combat even further. Following Owain's proclamation as Prince of Wales at Glyndyfrdwy the previous autumn, Tudur had taken part in the initial raids on Ruthin, the stronghold of Earl Grey, and other towns in the north and in the March.

Then, like several other initially keen followers such as the detestable Crach Ffinant, Tudur had thought better of the whole venture and had sought Henry IV's pardon. The pardon had been granted but it had only taken Tudur a month to realise that his conscience would not allow him to desert his brother's cause in that way, and he quickly returned to Owain's side and was now totally committed to supporting the rebellion in any way possible.

The following morning, I watched them go, a hard core of experienced, hardened warriors supplemented by scores of callow but eager young men, anxious to prove themselves and to gain the respect of Tudur and the other veterans as well as to share in the spoils of war. I wondered how they would feel in the depressing aftermath of battle. Some, no doubt, would share my sense of shame and disquiet, but none would admit to it. Warriors were warriors. They could be heroes or villains, but above all they were soldiers; there was no future for a soldier who admitted to a loss of self-respect or a sense of shame after doing what he had been trained to do. Now they were setting out to cause maximum damage to the Flemish settlers of south Pembrokeshire under the Red Dragon standard, led on this occasion by Tudur ap Gruffudd Fychan.

It was only a few weeks since the strange encounter between Henry Percy, known as Hotspur, the King's Justiciar for north Wales, and a force supposedly led by Glyndŵr, on the outskirts of Dolgellau. Hotspur's later boast to the King of complete victory was an empty one, for immediately after the battle his column had to beat a hasty retreat to Denbigh. I can reveal that neither Glyndŵr nor Hotspur were involved in the action, the English being led by the Earl of Arundel and the Welsh by Owain's lookalike brother, Tudur. I know this to be true because Owain and Hotspur were meeting in secret in a wood a few miles away from the battlefield, each accompanied by a senior retainer. I was Owain's retainer, and the purpose of the meeting was to explore possible English concessions, such as reaffirming the traditional rights of the *uchelwyr* and repealing the worst of the harsh penal laws. Agreement on these matters would allow Owain to break off the rebellion. This would have saved the loss of thousands of lives and avoided famine and ruination for many more during the following fifteen years. It would also have restored Henry IV's unchallenged rule in Wales, secured the collection of his taxes and saved the royal coffers from enormous depletion. Unfortunately, Bolingbroke's huge ego made him deaf to logical arguments and the last opportunity to secure a quick and peaceful outcome to the crisis was lost.

Now, as Tudur on a black destrier, and his war band, all mounted on shaggy mountain ponies, slowly dwindled down distant slopes, carrying war to the south west, I heaved a resigned sigh and joined the dozens of other well-wishers trudging back to the security of our Siambr Trawsfynydd base. Beyond the grassy ridge of Esgair y Ffordd was a deep valley through which flowed a small stream from the high land at the northern edge of the Pumlumon upland. The chamber was a rocky cleft in the hillside, opening out below into areas of flat land along the banks of a stream. It was well concealed from prying eyes until you were close to the cleft and certainly the best location for our purposes. Its existence would not be secret much longer, though, for our new herds of cattle and flocks of sheep were multiplying with every raid, and even the few shepherds in this near empty upland area would soon be talking freely to anyone they met about our presence here, and that of the captured livestock.

On reaching the entrance to Siambr Trawsfynydd we faced the obligatory challenge of the sentries before being allowed to ride our small, sure-footed mountain ponies down the steep sides of the valley, occasionally having to negotiate stretches of loose scree which presented no problems for our dexterous mounts. We were soon entering our base on the flat lands along the banks of the stream. My companions dispersed to their tents, but after dismounting and handing the pony into the care of a groom, I threaded my way past scores of roughly-fashioned tents and even more primitive shelters, heading for the centre of the encampment and Owain's large bivouac. Here the Red Dragon standard and the Black Lions rampant, traditional standard of the house of Powys Fadog, fluttered in the ever-present breeze. The two guards knew me well and did not challenge me. Instead, they moved aside and one of them held the entrance flap open for me to enter.

Owain was seated at a crudely-made table opposite a lean, flaxen-haired stranger who rose wearily to his feet. I noticed his travel-stained clothing and took him to be a messenger from Rhys ap Tudur and his men in the north west.

'*Bore da*, Gruffudd. So you went to see them off,' said Owain, also getting to his feet. 'This is our third major raid in just over a week.' He turned to the stranger. 'It means that four hundred and fifty men will have been involved in action, probably a third of them experiencing war for the first time. It will stand them in good stead for their first pitched battle against another army, an event which cannot be too far away.'

He turned back to me. 'Gruffudd – meet Tom Easton. Tom should have joined us for the march south but was unexpectedly held up by a skirmish with the English, near Llanrwst. That and, I dare say, some personal business.' Owain grinned at Easton who looked embarrassed for a moment. He quickly recovered though and came around the table offering me his hand. I grasped his hand and his grip was firm.

'*Henffych*,' I said somewhat hesitantly. He returned my

greeting but in an accent which confirmed my suspicion that the man was English. I took a step back, making it clear to him that I was putting some space between us.

My lord laughed aloud. 'I thought you would react with a cold reserve, Gruffudd. It is very rude of you.' He laughed again and I stared at them both, wondering what this was all about.

'Yes, Tom is an Englishman, but he is totally committed to our cause, I assure you.'

Suddenly I realised that this man was the Thomas Easton who had been pressed into service by the Tudur brothers of Anglesey when they captured Conwy Castle; the self-same Thomas who had played a leading role in the rescue of the condemned Welsh prisoners during their journey to Chester to be executed. I had been attending to the Lady Mared's safety in Sycharth at that time and so had not met him. I had always been deeply sceptical of such a man's trustworthiness. After all, he was an Englishman, and he had never denied his lineage. He had only been involved on our side in the capture and occupation of Conwy Castle because he had been catapulted into the situation by the Tudur brothers. It was also true that he had provided much needed expertise as a bowyer and fletcher, and had taken a nasty beating, as well as risking his life, in helping to secure the release of the eight condemned Welshmen. It was common knowledge that he was besotted with an Anglesey woman who had been a maid at the castle. Still, his apparent conversion to our cause was strange in my view. He seemed to have earned the trust and friendship of the Tudur brothers and the other Conwy Castle heroes, and had even learned to speak Welsh tolerably well. Nevertheless, I would be watching the fellow very carefully, particularly as he seemed to have won Owain over completely, and was accepted as a trusted member of our forces.

I wondered whether he had read my thoughts as we stood there, facing each other. He was considerably smaller, which should have put him at a disadvantage, for he had to look up at me; but he seemed oblivious to the difference in stature, looking me in the eye unflinchingly. When he spoke, his voice was steady and not unfriendly.

'So you are Gruffudd Fychan, Prince Owain's resident bard and the Princess of Wales's personal bodyguard. I'm told you are also a dangerous man with a battleaxe. Now that I have met you, I can readily believe that. Yet, you have a reputation for being a thinker, a poet and a musician too and I have heard some of your songs sung by other bards. They do you much credit, sire, and perhaps I will be lucky enough to hear you sing them in person one evening soon.'

With that, he turned to Owain to excuse himself and left to inspect the arrows that our fletchers were busily fashioning in the makeshift armoury.

'I can well understand your reserve, Gruffudd,' said Owain quietly. 'It mirrors my first reaction to the Englishman when he claimed to be a convert to the Welsh cause. But believe me, when you get to know him he will win you over just as he did me. He is a fine man, a skilled carpenter, bowyer and fletcher. Above all, he wears his heart on his sleeve and you will know soon enough if he disagrees with you on anything.'

'I hope, for all our sakes, that you are correct,' I responded, unconvinced. 'What news of the Lady Mared and the family? Did Tom Easton have any recent news of them?' I had been desperate to hear news of Mared ever since we had arrived in this dismal place, but had said nothing until now.

'You will be glad to hear that they are all alive and well. Mared and the girls are safe with my aunt and other members of the Tudur family on Anglesey. Madog has just turned seventeen and is a member of Rhys Tudur's war band, harassing the English in the north west?'

The news was good. Thus far the entire family was safe, for the eldest son, Gruffudd and the second son, Maredudd were serving with us. They had both featured prominently in our recent raid on Cardiganshire and northern Pembrokeshire and had returned unscathed.

'These Flemish who seem to have colonised the south west, Owain,' I said, 'It seems they have been there for a long time. I confess I know little of the affairs of our southern cousins. Having close connections with the royal line of Deheubarth on your mother's side, my lord, you must know something of their history.'

Owain's face darkened. 'As always, we have our English friends to thank for those unwelcome devils. They were originally invited to settle in the Rhos area of Pembrokeshire by Henry I as mercenary soldiers. Their mission was to curb and harass our countrymen in the area. Over time they established themselves as a community there and managed to force the native Welsh into the less fertile lands in the northern part of the county. Since the early twelfth century, and with the active support of successive Plantagenet kings, they have ruthlessly infiltrated as far as Gower to the east and northward into the fertile lands of south Cardiganshire. They have intermarried with English gentry and have formed a sizeable English-speaking colony in the south west of Wales, at heavy cost to our countrymen there. It is high time they had a dose of their own medicine, and I intend to repay their ruthlessness in kind. They will discover that the Welsh can bite back hard and often. That, in turn, will cause them to demand support from London, which will alarm Parliament and put more pressure on Bolingbroke.'

Three days later the elated raiding party returned. They drove large numbers of cattle and sheep ahead of them and seemed generally very pleased with themselves as they accepted our shouts of acclamation. There was also a sprinkling of dour and extremely angry Anglo-Flemish hostages, who were unceremoniously billeted securely under armed guards in a fenced compound close to our main encampment.

Tudur, the leader of the expedition, later asked Rhys Gethin to relate their adventures. A young man of few words and, unlike some of his fellows, a realist who was not prone to exaggeration, he was brief but eloquent. As he stood before Owain and his senior captains, he gave a short but fascinating account of the action.

On leaving the highlands Tudur had split his force into twenty groups of six to eight men, with each group travelling separately, mostly by night and giving towns a wide berth. The aim of this expedition had not been to attack castles and towns but to despoil the prosperous holdings of the rich Anglo-Flemish settlers, causing as much damage to life, property and crops as they could before stealing the livestock. By travelling discretely in small groups, they had managed to reach the southern reaches of Pembrokeshire without causing alarm. They had regrouped at a pre-arranged spot on one of the low Pembrokeshire hills before launching a dawn raid on the nearest settlement. Having created as much mayhem as they could on the startled and bewildered settlers, they had moved northward on a rampage, ravaging settlements from south to north almost as far as Cardiganshire. They also brought home the biggest haul of livestock so far, as well as targeting and capturing a select band of half-a-dozen hostages known to be worth their weight in ransom money.

Owain had schooled Rhys well in the art of addressing fellow soldiers, and in the skills of armed combat, and the acclaim following his report was deafening. Although admiring Rhys's command of his fellows' attention and the ruthless execution of Owain's orders, which could be attributed to him just as much as to Tudur, I could not help pondering how the Flemish would react to this spree of wholesale looting and killing. They were, after all, the descendants of tough, mercenary soldiers. I could not imagine that they would fail to react with some violence of their own.

11

ONE OF OUR two lookouts on Mynydd Hyddgen was the first to raise the alarm. Derfel Fychan was one of several hundred young lads who had flocked to Pumlumon as news of Owain's daring raids had filtered out to other parts of Wales. The nephew of Rhys Ddu, one of the most prominent of the west Wales noblemen and one of Owain's captains, Derfel was young and lacking in experience but, like most sons of *uchelwyr*, well trained as a horseman and in the use of weapons. He came hurtling into camp on a lathered pony, leapt to the ground and came running to Owain's bivouac where we were discussing plans for further attacks with the Prince's council of leaders and advisors.

I first heard the sound of loud shouting followed by a challenge from the guards. I quickly got to my feet and slipped out under the entrance flap to see who was responsible for such a commotion. It was Derfel being physically held by the guards until they could work out the cause of the young lad's excitement.

'Silence,' I roared. 'Who dares disturb our Prince in this unseemly fashion?'

'Master Gruffudd, please, you must hear me.'

'Alright, alright. But first you must calm down and behave like a man. You are not a child any more,' I replied in a disapproving tone. As I spoke I moved forward, indicating to the guards to release the chastened youngster. I put my arm around his shoulder.

'Now let us walk to somewhere a bit quieter and you can tell me what has disturbed you. Try to clear your mind and start from the beginning.'

It was only a few yards to the bank of the stream. We sat on a boulder and I listened with growing concern to his report.

'Huw Coch and I left camp at dawn this morning to do two days' duty as lookouts on Carn Hyddgen.'

This was the summit of Hyddgen mountain, where I had seen the eagle a fortnight before.

'When we got there we noticed that the even higher lookout post on Pumlumon Fawr would be of no use this morning, as the summit was surrounded by a band of thick cloud. Huw and I realised we would need to be especially watchful as we were the only lookouts able to see clearly down the long ribbon of the Rheidol river, running south in the valley below. Despite the dismal, cloudy morning, we could see clearly enough to follow the course of the Rheidol for some miles. The morning seemed unnaturally quiet. There was no birdsong, even. We chatted for a while before Huw gasped and pointed towards the river, as if struck dumb. Then I saw it; a column of armoured soldiers marching along the bank of the river towards us. It was several miles away but, as the column advanced, it became a long grey procession. Every so often the lines of marchers were interspersed with cohorts of mounted men. The great majority of them were on foot, though.'

'Can you guess, roughly, how many there are?'

'Difficult to say Master Gruffudd, but they must be at least twice as many as we are, and the best equipped army I have seen.' Derfel looked genuinely alarmed, though I knew he was doing his best not to show fear.

'Well done, Derfel. You and Huw have shown commendable devotion to duty by being so vigilant. We may all need to thank you later for saving our lives with this timely warning. Where is Huw, though? Is he safely back in camp?'

Derfel screwed up his face in exasperation. 'No, the idiot shouted at me to warn you all, and said he was going to take a closer look and report back with any useful information he could gather. I tried to warn him that his action would be foolhardy and dangerous, but he simply mounted his pony and set off down the mountainside, heading straight for the Flemings.'

'Brave, but very, very foolish,' I muttered. 'We can do nothing to help him now – but we can hurry back to Owain to prepare a warm welcome for the foreigners.'

We hurried back to report to Owain. This time the sentries saw the look on my face and moved aside smartly so we could enter unhindered. Owain looked up and stopped in mid-sentence. The others around the large, ungainly table also stared at us in silence.

'My Prince,' I said formally, 'I am sorry to interrupt you in this way. My friend, Derfel, has urgent news which requires our attention.'

'You are quite right to interrupt this meeting with urgent news,' Owain said quickly, eyeing the young lad keenly.

'Derfel, sire, is a nephew of your cousin Rhys Ddu of Deheubarth. He and another were the lookouts on Carn Hyddgen this morning. Now then, young man, relate the story you told me to your Prince and his council.'

Derfel started to kneel to his Prince but before he could complete the act Owain motioned him to rise.

'It is alright to stand, lad,' he said kindly. 'Just relax and tell us as you would tell your friends. After all, we are all friends here.'

The young man visibly relaxed and repeated his story, concentrating on his words and, I suspect, not fully appreciating the consternation on the faces of most of the assembled company as they realised the significance of his account.

'So, we are being hunted by a well-equipped, professional force at least twice our number with pikemen, cavalry and a large number of archers.'

Owain's voice was low and clipped. He was obviously thinking rapidly, trying to work out the best tactics to employ against a much superior force.

'You say that at least half of the archers were mounted as well? What sort of mounts did they have?'

Derfel screwed up his eyes, trying to remember. At last he said, 'The cavalry were mounted on typical, sturdy warhorses. Most of the archers had mountain ponies.'

'Damn!' Owain failed to hide his disappointment. The warhorses would be comparatively ineffective trying to charge across the marshes and soft gorse of these highlands. The archers, however, on their small but nimble ponies, unencumbered by heavy armour, could provide fast and dangerous sallies across the same hinterland. All of his captains immediately understood his frustration and murmured their own misgivings.

There was a sudden rush of feet outside and the guards issued loud challenges. Owain waited patiently for the fresh hubbub to subside. Then a guard led in a frightened-looking shepherd boy who stared in awe at Owain and sank to his knees.

Ever patient, Owain spoke kindly to the nervous young lad and bade him stand.

'What is it, lad? Do not be afraid. You are safe here. Now, what is your message and who sent you to me?'

'W-well, *fy Nhywysog*. I am called Trefor. Mmm-my father Tysul Talsarnau, a ssh-shepherd and supporter of your cause, has sent me in great haste to tell you that the English and Flemish of Pembrokeshire have sent a large force along the banks of the Rheidol to attack you. They have also sent another force to attack you from the north, cutting off any chance of retreat. There are a thousand men in the southern army and another five hundred coming to surprise you from the north.'

There was a short, shocked silence broken by Owain.

'Thank you, Trefor. You have been very brave coming here to tell me. I already know about the army approaching from the south, but are you quite sure that there is another force approaching from the north?'

'Yes, sire. I saw them with my own eyes and ran home to tell my father. He said you must be told at once and sent me to you immediately.'

'I am very grateful for your warning, Trefor. Will you thank your father for me?'

He turned to the guard who, like the rest of us, was standing transfixed, staring at the youngster.

'See that this brave boy is given plenty to eat before he sets off for home. Keep well away from any path which would expose you to the enemy, Trefor, for if they catch you they will want information from you, and will torture you to get it. And be sure to give your father my warmest regards.'

'I will follow your advice, sire,' the boy responded with a nervous smile. 'My father says that in a few years I will be grown up. Then, I can choose to fight in your army if you will have me.'

'You are a young man of spirit, Trefor. Come to me when your father thinks you are ready and I will gladly accept you into my service.'

Once the boy had left accompanied by the burly guard, Owain returned to his seat at the table. We all followed suit with several talking across each other in near panic.

'Silence,' he thundered, and there was an immediate and expectant silence. 'I will not have officers in any army of mine who panic at the first whiff of danger,' he said evenly, his voice taking on a menacing, yet strangely reassuring tone.

'There is no time for discussion or argument,' he continued. 'We are hemmed in to the south and to the north by enemy forces. They are well equipped and appear to be professional armies. They also outnumber us by around three to one. I do not have to tell you that they represent a very dangerous threat to us and we must act immediately. Tudur, I want you to take eighty mounted archers to meet the Flemings to the south. Obviously you will not engage them directly. You must use the terrain, which will become increasingly difficult for such a large body of men to negotiate, and use any opportunity to halt or slow down their advance. Use your arrows sparingly but to good effect. We will need a plentiful supply of arrows to help our main defence effort. Rhys Gethin, you will take fifty mounted archers and devise similar tactics to halt or slow down the advance of the northern force. The same rules of engagement apply, Rhys. No foolhardy heroics, please. I want you all back hale and unharmed by nightfall. I shall be at Carn Hyddgen with our main force by then, having set up a defensible position on the summit. Finally, I turn to you, Ednyfed ap Siôn. As well as organising medical support for all our fighting men, I would like you to handle the immediate evacuation of our remaining horses from here to the caves we have identified at the northern end of this valley. Also, you will need to impress upon all non-combatants – cooks, grooms, the foolish wives and girlfriends who have chosen to follow their menfolk to war, and any other hangers-on, that they must leave immediately. They, too, can find temporary shelter in the network of caves we have discovered further up the valley. Warn them that they are on no account to return here until we seek them out after the battle. If they have heard nothing after, say, five days, they are to disperse and return to their homes.'

There was a grim silence as we all pondered that final allusion to the possibility of defeat. Defeat on Carn Hyddgen would mean certain death for all of us. There is no means of escape from a mountain top surrounded by an enemy.

'However,' Owain continued quickly, looking each one of us in the eye in turn and raising his voice slightly, 'my expectation is of complete victory over the Flemish barbarians.'

'To victory!' we all shouted in reply, before trooping out to ready the army for its first major battle, trying hard to push the daunting odds to the back of our minds.

Soon the whole camp was a hive of activity. A stranger could have been forgiven for seeing it as panic-stricken and desperate. Closer observation would have shown it to be a highly-organised, if hurried, exit from what had, until now, been a safe haven for Glyndŵr and his followers.

An hour later the first detachment of archers was pacing out an area covering the whole of the small plateau at the summit of Carn Hyddgen, seeking to organise it as best they could as a ridout for the expected Anglo-Flemish assault. In another hour all of Owain's army, apart from the one hundred and thirty mounted archers sent to slow down the Flemish advances, was occupying the plateau with officers directing the efforts to build stretches of low, dry-stone walls in strategic spots where the natural cover was non-existent.

It was early evening when the lookout spotted Tudur and his contingent of archers approaching from the south. They scrambled their way up the slopes of Hyddgen leading their blown ponies. All were in good spirits for they had surprised the enemy at a ford where they had to cross the river Rheidol. Hidden amongst gorse and tall reeds some seventy yards from the near river bank, they had killed an estimated two dozen soldiers as the enemy forded the river. Like many soldiers who wear heavy armour in battle, the Flemings had discarded it on the march because of the summer heat and the pain and discomfort caused by the chafing of the heavy metal trappings. The attack of the Welsh longbow men was a total surprise and half of the victims were dead in the water before anyone realised they were under attack. A second volley had claimed the lives of at least another dozen and injured many more. An English voice from across the river shouted to the stunned survivors to return to the other bank and take cover. Meanwhile, Tudur had halted the vicious volleys of his archers so that, when the enemy returned a volley of their own, it would be difficult to judge where exactly to direct their arrows.

The Anglo-Flemish advance had now come to a complete standstill. Every twenty minutes or so they would make half-hearted attempts to ford the river, but a few well-chosen targets would be felled as soon as they showed themselves and the stalemate would be re-asserted. Eventually, Tudur and his men became aware of noise and activity taking place just out of their sight and Tudur realised that a large body of lightly-armoured, mounted archers was being assembled for a major effort to ford the river and attack him and his men. More than three hours had elapsed and Tudur knew that they had done what was needed and that Owain and his men were by now in position on Carn Hyddgen. He could see no logical reason to try and counter the coming onslaught. They would probably be overrun in any case and he was honour bound to keep as many as possible of his archers alive and capable of active duty for the coming battle. They withdrew quietly, before the enemy had readied their powerful force for the assault.

While Tudur was reporting to Owain and his command council on the events of the day, Rhys Gethin returned with his fifty archers. They had managed to ambush the leading column of the northern army in a narrow defile and rapid volleys from his archers had killed at least sixty of the enemy and injured as many as thirty more. Rhys, too, had managed to check the enemy advance for several hours until a detachment of enemy troops struggled across the boggy terrain of an adjacent valley to get behind him. Sudden awareness of their peril came when a quarrel from the crossbow of an over-eager Flemish archer whistled past Rhys's head, missing him by inches. He and his men hurriedly dived for cover as a hail of quarrels came hissing towards them. All their targets had moved marginally before the crossbow men had released their surprise volley, so none of the Welshmen was hit.

Rhys quickly ordered everyone back to the horses, taking advantage of the comparatively slow reload time for crossbows. The next salvo was ineffective as Rhys and his men were some distance away by then, galloping up the valley and out of danger. The great advantage of the longbow over the crossbow, of course, is that an archer can release arrows from a longbow at a staggering rate of up to ten per minute while the crossbow man can manage only three quarrels at best in the same time.

At the reunion on Carn Hyddgen, both parties of archers were acclaimed by their leaders and their comrades. Both groups had succeeded in halting the advancing enemy troops from north and south for several valuable hours, as well as inflicting up to a hundred casualties before returning safely, having suffered no losses of their own.

Dawn broke the following morning, merely turning black of night into a cheerless, chilly grey. Heavy clouds swirled around the highlands of Pumlumon forming a thick, damp fog. I got up early, and momentarily startled Arthur ap Gwyn and Llŷr Llechwedd on sentry duty as they warmed their hands by a stuttering fire and exchanged unflattering comments about the nature of summer in the area. For a while we chatted quietly, with both expressing misgivings about the daunting military situation we had been caught up in. Suddenly, Arthur sprang to his feet, at once alert and reaching for the pike which was never far from his side. Llŷr, reacting to his comrade's actions, was also on his feet in an instant, sword drawn.

'Who goes there?' Arthur called sharply. 'Why are you about at this ungodly hour? Speak or feel the point of my pike in your belly!'

'All is well, Arthur. It is only me, Derfel.'

'What on earth are you doing walking around so early? Would you not be better off, even in your makeshift bed?'

'I could not sleep for worrying about my friend, Huw. There has been no word from him since he rode off to take a closer look at the Flemings yesterday morning. That's not like Huw. I'm afraid he may have been captured... or worse...'

'And now you are thinking of going to look for him?' I asked quietly.

'Yes, that is exactly what I'm going to do,' Derfel said firmly, tossing his head defiantly as if expecting opposition to his plan.

'Derfel, there is no one on this mountain who would not willingly join in a hunt for your friend,' I said kindly. 'You are quite rightly worried, for he has embarked on a very dangerous journey. However, as a soldier in Glyndŵr's army, you have to think about the bigger picture before you decide what to do.'

'What bigger picture?' Derfel's voice was brittle and dismissive. 'What could possibly be bigger or more important than rescuing my friend?'

'Your concern for your friend does you credit. However, you are kin to a family of chieftains, and chieftains have to make decisions based on the greater good of their communities. You, Derfel, are now one of five hundred or so soldiers of Prince Owain IV of Wales. No matter how devoted you are to Huw, your first and overriding duty at present is to ensure the safety and well-being of your Prince and his trapped army. I know it is difficult, but you are now a full grown man and a nephew of Rhys Ddu, one of Glyndŵr's most senior captains. You have to show you are a true kinsman of his. I'm sure that Huw, if he were here now, would echo my words.'

As I spoke, I saw the lad's face change through a sequence

of expressions as he came to understand the situation; from initial annoyance which changed quickly to shock, then a new realisation of what was expected of him and finally a shamed acceptance which tugged at my heart. Growing up in a war zone is quick and often painful.

'Thank you, Gruffudd. It is not an easy thing to accept, but what you say is true.'

'If it is any consolation to you,' I responded quietly, 'I will ensure that the scouts we send out shortly will be briefed to keep a sharp lookout for any clues which may help us find your friend.'

Derfel swallowed hard, trying to keep his emotions in check. He nodded, then turned quickly away before striding back into the swirling mist.

'If I may say so, Master Gruffudd – that was very skilfully handled,' Arthur murmured, a measure of respect in his voice.

I smiled at him and made my way back to my tent, my heart full of admiration for young Derfel's brave but painful acceptance of the harsh realities of our situation.

Owain sent out a dozen scouts to locate the enemy; six south towards the river Rheidol, the others along the Hengwm Valley, in search of the detachment travelling from the north. By midday, ten had returned with interesting information. The northern enemy force had headed straight for Siambr Trawsfynydd, confirming that their intelligence had been sound. They were obviously surprised and annoyed that we had second-guessed their intentions and vacated the camp by the stream. They fired our tents and huts but failed to find a living soul, for we had moved our hostages, camp followers and our horses several miles away to the cave area and the Flemings were not aware of that for, having destroyed everything they could, they turned back and started across the long, marshy and tiring route towards Carn Hyddgen. The other four scouts reported that the main enemy army was making steady progress towards our position on Carn Hyddgen from the south. We were beginning to be concerned at the non-arrival of the last two scouts when we spotted them starting the long climb up the southern slopes of Hyddgen. One of them was leading a third pony with what appeared to be a body draped across the saddle.

I happened to be with the sentries as the returning scouts finally arrived. One of them was Gwyn Trefnant, an archer whom I knew well. He was grim-faced as he walked his pony towards me.

'The bastards have made a fine mess of the young lad, Gruffudd. We found him in the wood, with his pony grazing near the body. The cruel sods tortured him to death. He must have held out through hours of torment before he finally died, poor devil.'

Gwyn dismounted and he and I walked over to the crumpled corpse lying across the third pony's back. The animal looked forlorn and stood perfectly still. Gwyn lifted the head and I gasped in shock as I found myself inches from sightless, scorched eye sockets. The Flemings had used hot irons to burn out Huw's eyes. Gwyn allowed the head to sink back to its upside down position and lifted the youngster's left hand. The tips of thumb and four fingers were caked with dried blood. They had removed his fingernails in what must have been a slow, agonising experience for the boy. Finally, the scout lifted Huw's right hand to reveal a deep laceration to his wrist.

'That was probably done last, so that he would bleed to

death,' said Gwyn Trefnant with a slow sigh. 'We will never know whether or not they broke him and gained whatever information they required. Either way, he was a very, very brave young man.'

I nodded, not trusting myself to speak. It was difficult to comprehend how any human being could inflict such calculated savagery on a fellow human.

'Gwyn, I want you to take the body quickly to Ednyfed ap Siôn for immediate burial. I do not want young Derfel Fychan, Rhys Ddu's nephew, to see what those sons of whores did to his close friend.'

The two scouts hurried away with the corpse of the heroic youngster. The mist was thinning out, increasing the possibility that they might be spotted by others causing a noisy reaction which, in turn, could bring Derfel to the scene. I really did not want the lad to witness the horrors inflicted upon his late friend. Fortunately the body was delivered to Ednyfed's makeshift sickbay without arousing a sensation and I knew that our master physician would deal discretely with the situation from there on.

Within half an hour the June sun finally broke through, quickly burning the remaining mist away and the army, under the calm direction of Owain, took up defensive positions around the summit's perimeter, in readiness for the arrival of the Anglo-Flemish forces. We did not have long to wait. We first became aware of the sound of a solitary drum sending out a slow, steady beat for the soldiers to march to. The sound was measured and unhurried and its deliberate, constant rendering seemed like a portend of doom booming up the mountainside. Our trepidation increased as the enemy came into view, and many of the men gasped in shock as a seemingly never-ending, double row of heavily-armoured troops slowly encircled the base of Carn Hyddgen. This was the larger force from the south. As soon as they had taken up their positions the drum stopped. The menacing silence was soon broken by the sound of another drum a mile or so to the north and, shortly after, more heavily-armoured troops took up positions to reinforce the first arrivals. It was a daunting sight. We were outnumbered by at least three to one by soldiers with more and better armour than ours; many of our men had no armour at all – with only their weapons and wooden bucklers to protect themselves.

Most of their army had been ordered to rest, for the majority began to unbuckle their armour and find places to sit down. Only a sizeable minority kept their armour on and stood within easy reach of weapons to assure us that they would be ready for us, if we did the unthinkable, and elected to attack. They had realised that with our much smaller army, we would not risk taking them on in an all-out frontal attack while we had the advantage of holding the high ground.

After an hour or so an enemy officer, clutching a white flag, detached himself from his companions and started to climb up the north-western approach to Carn Hyddgen, where irregular rocky outcrops interspersed with tussocks of grass covered the steep hillside. The man stopped when he got within shouting distance and hailed us.

'I am Captain Jan de Groote. My commander, Sir William Beauchamp, wishes to parley with the rebel, Owen Glendower. This should happen quickly so that he can surrender to a much superior force immediately, before any more blood is shed in what is a hopeless rebellion.'

We all turned towards the area where Owain stood,

listening carefully to the messenger. He quickly strode forward and jumped onto a boulder on the edge of our perimeter defences and shouted his reply.

'Captain de Groote. You can tell Sir William that if he wishes to have a civil discussion with Owain IV, Prince of Wales, he can do so on the spot on which you now stand. However, he will need to show due respect to the Prince of Wales's position as the *Tywysog* of this land, and he will need to forget any thoughts of surrender… unless, of course, he is ready to surrender his own forces, which are guilty of trespass on a Welsh prince's lands. I will require only Sir William and his senior commanders to surrender their swords. The rest of you will be allowed to return safely to your homes.'

There was a roar of approval and laughter from our ranks and the Flemish captain stared at Owain, his face etched in disbelief.

'Sire, is that truly what you wish me to report to Sir William as your honest answer?'

'Most certainly, de Groote. Now be off with you. You can also inform Sir William that the Prince of Wales does not take kindly to being kept waiting.'

Red-faced with annoyance, the captain clenched his teeth, and turned his horse around without another word before guiding it back down the slope. Owain, too, came bounding back to our lines and, brushing past me, muttered, 'Cheeky bastards', then stopped and clapped me on the shoulders, grinning all over his face. Half an hour later he was ready to return to the meeting point.

'Come, axeman,' he said lightly. 'Come and be my bodyguard for a change.'

Sir William was already coming up the hill on foot with

a tall swordsman at his side. When we finally came face-to-face I could see that the enemy leader was a short, pot-bellied man with lank, greasy hair. He exuded self-importance. This trait, together with the stark physical contrast between him and the tall swordsman at his side, was so comical that I had great difficulty in keeping a straight face. Keeping my laughter in check was made all the more difficult in the knowledge that Owain was having similar difficulty, as he struggled to turn what sounded suspiciously like the beginnings of a laugh into a short cough. The swordsman glared at us with disdain, slowly moving his neck from side to side as if loosening his muscles in readiness for rapid physical action. Sir William glanced across at his companion and, to my dismay, promptly emulated the neck exercises. Again Owain cleared his throat in a determined effort to hide his mirth, while I concentrated on unbuckling my shoulder belt, releasing the cover of my battleaxe. I glared at the swordsman as I loosened the handle of the weapon in its sheath and placed it gently to rest against a rock. I was conscious of Sir William looking at me like a startled rabbit.

'Well, Sir William, you wanted to talk.' Owain made a determined effort to end the charade.

'Not to talk, but to state the terms of your surrender. You, sir, are a thief and a renegade, denounced by the King as a traitor.'

'Enough, Beauchamp. Another word and I shall skewer your fat belly to the ground on which you stand. I am Owain, by the grace of God, Prince of Wales, and I will not tolerate insults from you or any other supporter of a man who has no right to the throne of England, or any other throne.' Owain spoke in a measured, matter-of-fact manner which, nevertheless, was heavy with menace. 'If we are going to discuss surrender at all, it will be the terms upon which I shall relieve you of your sword,' he concluded.

Sir William found it impossible to hide his fear as he paled and shuffled closer to his swordsman who, in turn, placed his hand on the hilt of his sword.

'I am…' He paused in an effort to master the tremor in his voice. 'I am the Earl of Pembroke and the… Jus… Justiciar of south Wales. King Henry has instructed me to bring you before him to answer to charges of treason, murder, unlawfully attacking his subjects, stealing their possessions and abduction.'

'And I, also, have an instruction for you. As the lawful and only sovereign Prince of Wales I want you to inform Bolingbroke that he no longer has jurisdiction over any part of Wales. Therefore, neither I, nor my people are in any way subject to English law. It will be a painful lesson for him, but he will no longer be entitled to collect taxes from my subjects and I will wage war on him to ensure that Wales will not be a land to be used as a means of replenishing English royal coffers.'

Owain had hardly completed the sentence before he motioned me to collect my axe and join him as he turned his back on the Englishmen and strode purposefully back to our encampment on the summit.

After a moment's stunned silence Sir William bleated, 'You are mad… q-quite mad. Do you not realise that we outnumber you three to one? Can you not see that you have lost this battle before it is fought?'

We kept on walking, pointedly ignoring him.

12

I AWOKE TO the sounds of hundreds running around in panic, of voices shouting, some screaming in pain, yells of anger, fear and bewilderment. As I rushed to the entrance of my tent I thought, for a brief moment, that we had somehow been transported into the bowels of hell. My comrades were running frantically in all directions, colliding with each other and mouthing obscenities. There was a weird, hissing noise from above and I looked up into a strangely bizarre blue sky to see hail upon hail of arrows and crossbow bolts hurtling down upon us. I could see comrades collapsing all around me and I roared my anger and frustration at our lack of defences against attack from the skies, wondering at the same time how this could be happening when the enemy had camped well beyond bowshot. Then Owain and some officers arrived holding their bucklers above their heads and screaming at the men to fetch bucklers to try and shield themselves from the murderous onslaught. Though not designed to stop quarrels and arrows, the wooden shields would afford some protection. I hastily ran back to my tent to collect my own buckler and rushed out again to see some semblance of discipline being restored by the officers, while Rhys Gethin angrily called on all available archers to man the perimeter defences in order to subject the enemy to a dose of his own medicine.

'Hurry up, lads. String those bows and follow me. If those

bastards are close enough to attack us – then they are close enough to be attacked.'

The descending clouds of projectiles thinned out considerably as we returned fire. It was obvious that large numbers of enemy archers had moved up much closer to our camp under cover of darkness to launch their concentrated attack. Now, in daylight, they were badly exposed and soon our own volleys of arrows were mowing them down mercilessly. In a very short time our attackers were in full retreat, many still being felled as they ran.

Our brief celebrations soon fizzled out. Although we had killed many of our attackers, for the mountainside was littered with lifeless bodies over an area of several hundred yards, our own losses were even heavier. Many of our dead had been killed while still half asleep, and many more had been killed or injured before they could reach their bucklers. Some had even died from quarrels and arrows driving right through their bucklers.

A pall of sadness and shock hung over the encampment for the remainder of that day as our comrades attended to the wounded and the dying. A furious Owain held a council of war with his captains that afternoon. He was obviously angry with himself rather than with anyone else.

'Before we begin,' Owain began in a subdued voice. 'I want to apologise to the living and to the dead for what was an appalling error on my part last night. I completely failed to anticipate the surprise attack this morning. Any worthwhile leader should have realised that they might use the darkness to sneak up closer for a surprise attack. I can assure you, it will never happen again under my command. I forgot the most basic rules of warfare – never underestimate the enemy leader. He cut such a ridiculous figure with his posturing yesterday that I was lulled into a foolish complacency. As a result we have suffered losses we could ill afford.'

'I think you are being unfair on yourself in trying to take the blame for what has happened,' Ednyfed ap Siôn said briskly. 'We are all in this and none of us foresaw the danger either, or we would have raised our concerns with you. It is also reasonable to ask what our sentries were doing throughout last night. How is it that so many of the enemy managed to close in on us without revealing themselves by sight or sound?'

There were murmurs of support for this view from around the table and, despite insisting again that the blame lay with him, I could see signs of relief on Owain's face as he moved on to talk about our casualties.

'We counted fifty-seven dead, shortly after the attack. That number has now risen to sixty-four, with seven of the injured having died as well. We have a further twenty-six injured, of whom twenty are not considered to be seriously hurt. Nevertheless we have at least seventy fewer fighters than we did yesterday, and another twenty-odd who may, or may not, be fit to fight when the time comes.'

'I say we should mount an all-out attack of our own tomorrow while we still have our strength, and give them hell,' Rhys Gethin snapped, his frustration boiling over.

'No,' Rhys Ddu responded firmly. 'Pitting four hundred or so against fourteen hundred men in a do-or-die assault would be nothing short of suicide.'

There was a chorus of agreement for this view. Rhys Gethin tossed his head in annoyance and rested his face in his hands, elbows on the table, a picture of despair. A fiery bundle of aggression, Rhys did not always allow his head to rule his big heart. Everyone could sense that, in reality, the young firebrand had identified this situation as an impossible one, but had needed to find an outlet to let off steam.

'I commend you for your courage, Rhys,' Owain said, 'but I think you know, in your heart, that your suggestion is not a realistic one, at least not for the moment. The men need a day or two to get over the shock of losing so many friends and comrades. In truth, I believe they also need to feel the urgency and desperation of starving men before they will be ready for a do-or-die battle.' He paused, watching the shock registering on the faces around him. 'You may well find my words shocking, but I believe they have some force. It is also possible as the days wear on, that our opponents will become supremely confident – over-confident even – convinced that soon all they will need do is saunter up to the summit, and overwhelm a body of men too weak to put up a real fight.'

We went to our beds that night convinced that none of us would live to see another week. The sentries, meanwhile, went to their posts fired-up and vigilant. They had no intention of allowing the events of the previous night to be repeated.

The following morning we awoke again to a cloudless, blue sky but there were no more enemy attacks. Instead, we all began to feel pangs of hunger and thirst gnawing at us. Our food and water supplies were very low. In our haste, we had only managed to carry small quantities of food and water with us from Siambr Trawsfynydd, and no one had really considered that our confrontation with the Flemings would last more than two or three days. We had severely rationed our supplies from the outset, but it was clear that in another two days we would reach a crippling crisis, particularly when the water ran out. I cursed the pleasant morning sunshine, knowing full well that, as the day wore on, the summer heat would bake us on that barren mountain top, adding to our thirst and increasing our exhaustion. I thought of all the cold, damp days we had endured on the Pumlumon highlands. How ironic that the much anticipated sun had now arrived when we would have given anything for the mists and the rain to return.

We ate our only ration for the day in the cool of the evening. A mood of tangible depression had descended on us all. The usual joking and harmless baiting of companions had gone, to be replaced by a morose silence, occasionally broken by the sounds of squabbles and one or two more serious quarrels, where participants had to be separated by members of Owain's personal guard, *Y Cedyrn*.

Later, Owain called a meeting of his senior captains, together with Ednyfed and me. There was a look of utter dejection on most of the faces around the table. I studied the individuals, wondering who would have reserves of strength and determination, and who might possibly wilt when the going got unbearably bad. Rhys Ddu, solid and dependable as a rock, sat grave but by no means cowed; the firebrand Rhys Gethin's face was set in its usual pugnacious form while his friend and Owain's son, Maredudd, was staring with some pride at his father and looking determined. Tudur, tough and durable, gave little away; Dafydd, Owain's eldest son was struggling to look determined but his eyes revealed worry and agitation. Hywel ap Gronw regarded the company with commendable calm, even managing a tight smile; and Ednyfed, the experienced medic, sat patiently waiting for the meeting to begin, as if tomorrow would be just another day without a cloud on the horizon. I wondered, briefly, if others were assessing me and whether my face was betraying my inner feelings. It was not a comfortable thought. Meanwhile Owain, though appearing a little careworn, was surprisingly upbeat in voice and demeanour as he called the meeting to order.

'My friends, I have brought you together, as you can probably guess, because we have reached the moment when we have to take decisive action. As you are all too aware, any further delay will find us too weak to fight. Now, we all know the weakness of our situation so I will not dwell on that. I would rather consider the enemy's state of mind. I don't know about you, but if I were one of Beauchamp's lieutenants, I would be feeling pretty confident that this stand-off is well nigh over. I would be confident that the rebel force, starving and thirsty, is finished as a fighting force. I would be telling my men that we only need wait another day before we take our time to climb to the summit and casually finish off the remnants of Glyndŵr's exhausted army. I suspect that the entire Anglo-Flemish force, from their leader down to their least experienced foot soldier, is fair brimming with over confidence. Well, gentlemen, I plan to give them the shock of their lives, and this is how we will do it.'

An hour later, the officers were assembling every able-bodied man to be addressed by Owain. It was a slow task, for they all seemed consumed by lethargy and physical weakness, convinced that their time had come and that nothing could save them from the jaws of death, whether by starvation, or by the wrath of the Flemings. When their Prince came to stand before them, the officers moved the men back so that the front rank was placed some fifteen paces distant. Before addressing them, Owain drew his great sword and marched to within five paces of the nearest soldiers. Then, with determined deliberation, he plunged the point of his blade into the hard ground so that, notwithstanding the parched earth, it sank several inches. When he released his grip, turned and marched crisply back to his previous position, back straight, head held high, the sword's handle was still humming with vibration from the force of his action. It was dusk, and two braziers had been lit and placed some yards to either side of Owain. It was quite a clever ploy, for as dusk changed to darkness our leader cut an awe-inspiring figure – handsome, strong and determined. Some of the more superstitious among us must have wondered whether all the tales told about him, of his powers as a magician, able to control the very elements to help him fight his enemies, were true. We had heard that many among the English, some in high places, were beginning to believe in his superhuman powers and as I looked at his countenance taking on a myriad expressions in the flickering light of the flaming braziers, it was easy to imagine him as the embodiment of some spirit from the house of Lucifer himself, come to erase the Flemings from the face of the earth. Even to the less fanciful among us he seemed, in the light of the flames, to have suddenly grown larger and his whole being, the flowing locks, regal bearing and broad shoulders, spoke of certain and triumphal victory, before he had even said a word. There was an inexplicable aura about him which projected him as every inch a credible incarnation of the long-prophesied *Mab Darogan*. When he eventually started addressing the troops, their enthusiasm for his air of invincibility persuaded them to reject their earlier despair. The surge of new-found confidence that replaced it was a palpable, all-encompassing experience, such as I had never witnessed before.

'I suppose that like me, most of you have wandered over to the perimeter in darkness to look down on the enemy cooking fires and thought how wonderful it would be to get your hands on some of the meats and other good things you can smell, wafting up to your nostrils.'

Owain's voice was firm and conversational in a way which made everyone present feel that he was being spoken to as an equal. It was a reassuring tone – somehow comforting yet strengthening one's resolve at the same time.

'Can I begin by asking you, no matter how much you may like, or dislike, what I have to say, to refrain from any shouting or laughing aloud. We do not want the enemy to hear loud voices, joyous or otherwise, because we are all meant to be too weak to stand, let alone shout, by now. I want them to continue in that belief.' He paused to allow a low chuckle to ripple through the ranks.

'I would also ask you all to sit, for we must conserve all our energy for what I have in mind.'

They all seemed relieved and took their chance to sit quickly and with minimum disruption. As the braziers again momentarily brightened, Owain's face was thrown into sharp relief and the yellow eyes roved quickly over his listeners, his expression a study in gritty determination.

'My faithful friends, you know as well as I do that tomorrow we face our most difficult test yet, by far. By nightfall we will all either be dead, and our struggle for freedom ended, finished – possibly forever, or we will be celebrating a glorious and historic victory which will send shivers through the King and all the great English lords in London and in the March. Such a victory will be hailed all over Wales and Welshmen who, until now have not joined us because they had little confidence in our ability to win the struggle, will flock to our banner, and even Bolingbroke will realise that we are a real threat to him. However, if we lose, then apart from the heartache of losing fathers, brothers, husbands and lovers, our women will face harrowing poverty as will our children, who will be brought up in a world where, as adults, they will have no rights and will be treated as little better than slaves.'

Here Owain quickly raised his hand to stifle the growls of anger, as his men reacted to the worst-case scenario he had depicted.

'But fear not, my friends, for I and your commanders have worked out a plan we firmly believe can bring us victory tomorrow. To do so I have to stress, we will all have to fight as we have never fought in our lives till now. I would like you to cast your minds back to last September, when I was proclaimed Prince of Wales. Following the proclamation, which many of you attended, we made our way to the old hill fort of Caer Drewyn where, two hundred years ago, the largest Welsh army ever assembled under the joint leadership of the leading Welsh princes and lords of that time – including Owain Gwynedd, Owain Cyfeiliog of Powys and the Lord Rhys of Deheubarth – routed the English King Henry II, and thirty thousand men. The English and their French and Scottish allies were forced to retreat through the Berwyn mountains back into England, harried all the way by the jubilant, combined Welsh army. I spoke of that famous victory at Caer Drewyn on my Proclamation Day. I now want to mention another battle, which took place only a few days before that famous victory. The massive army of Henry II included forces commandeered from Normandy, Gascony, and Anjou, as well as Scotland and England. The English King was so confident in the power of his army that, rather than follow the traditional route along the north Wales coast, he decided to march from Shrewsbury straight over the Berwyn mountains and up the Ceiriog Valley. This unusual move surprised the Welsh and Owain Gwynedd, together with his brother Cadwaladr, and the men of Gwynedd realised that they had to hold this mighty army for some days, until the forces of Powys and Deheubarth could join them. Outnumbered by more than six to one, Owain Gwynedd ambushed the leading columns of Henry's forces in the upper Ceiriog Valley at Adwy'r Beddau, the aptly named Pass of the Graves. During the Battle of Crogen, as it became known, the men of Gwynedd fought with such ferocity and valour that the enemy was forced to give ground and the King barely escaped with his life. By the time they had regrouped some days later, they found themselves facing a surprisingly large Welsh army on Caer Drewyn and… well… you all know the rest of the story. Like us tomorrow, Owain Gwynedd and his men went into battle against overwhelming odds knowing that they were in a desperate struggle, not simply to avoid being killed, but to ensure the safety of their families, who would have been massacred if the enemy had cut its way through the pass. And remember, for years afterwards, a "Son of Crogen" described any Welsh warrior of exceptional courage.

'And now it is our time to surprise the enemy, your time and mine. Remember when you move out tomorrow morning to scatter those foreigners down below, that you are all that stands between your families, your loved ones and a nightmare existence. Our kin will be made to pay a bitter price for our rebellion and none of us wants that. Finally, remember that we are very different from the forces waiting down there who would love to kill us all. They are here because they have been pressed into service. But every single one of you is a volunteer. You all identify with our historic Golden Dragon banner through a deep sense of kinship and duty to our ancient race.

'You are here because you want to be a free people, not vassals of foreigners. You want me as your *Tywysog*; you want to be on equal terms with your neighbour; you want a return to the good Welsh laws of Hywel Dda; you want to live in a society with justice to protect you and yours; you want to pay reasonable taxes based on what you can afford; and you want your heirs to be educated in your own language and to conduct your business through the medium of Welsh. In short, you want all the rights which a free people take for granted.

'Tomorrow, half an hour before dawn you will assemble here again in full battle order and your commanders will outline our battle plan, concentrating on what will be expected of you. It will probably be different to any combat situation you have experienced before. I will not say any more now, except to tell you that all archers will leave their bows and arrows in camp and present themselves armed, simple, with sword and buckler. The same goes for the pikemen. Why? Well, the whole idea tomorrow will be to get in amongst the enemy, giving no quarter, denying them time to think. It will not be pretty, for it will be an ugly, bloody contest fought at close quarters, and the short swords of the archers and the pikemen will be ideal – much more effective than the Flemings's longer swords. You have all heard of the Romans who ruled over us many centuries ago. The chief weapon of the Roman legions was the *gladus*, a sword probably even shorter than ours, and they conquered most of the known world! I shall want the axemen to use their battleaxes, for the axe is another savage, destructive weapon at close quarters. Tomorrow my friends, we must be prepared to fight to the last gasp, for it is a fight we have to win. I am confident that generations to come will remember the Battle of Hyddgen, just as we remember Crogen. Who knows, they may, in future, celebrate an exceptionally brave Welsh warrior by describing him as a true son of Hyddgen. That, of course, depends on your hunger for victory; your desire to prove your worth as warriors; your courage in defending your kin; and your absolute determination to out-think and out-fight those foreign curs who are down there even now eating good Welsh lamb and Welsh pork and drinking Welsh ale, while we sit here starving and desperate for water. In a few hours' time I will meet you here to lead you down this mountainside to give those bastards the thrashing they deserve.'

Owain walked over to where we, his officers, were sitting near the theatrical dance of the brazier flames. We all stood in unspoken admiration for the man, though I noticed with concern that as he approached his shoulders seemed to droop as I embraced him. I saw that his face was ashen and he stumbled and would have fallen had I not held him, though I managed to turn him away from the other officers so that they could not see his sudden weakness.

The effect of his words on the men was electrifying for, as he stepped out of the light, there was a low but powerful reactive growl from them all, clearly indicating a new-found confidence and determination. When they got up and walked away to their sleeping quarters, there was a new confidence about them. They went with shoulders straight and heads held high and my heart was filled with pride. They were my fellow *Cymry* and I knew that whatever the morrow might bring, I was serving with a small but very special army, under a hugely charismatic leader.

13

I GOT DRESSED hurriedly. It was exceptionally cold for a June morning, even allowing for the pre-dawn hour. I slid the scabbard of my short sword onto my belt and secured the buckle. Then I slid my sword into the scabbard, moving it back and fore a few times to ensure its smooth release when required. I would not be bothering with my buckler for, like all the other axemen, I would need both hands to handle my twin-headed axe which had, over several days, been honed into two keen edges which shone in the flickering light of my candle. I hefted the weapon experimentally, trying to ignore the sharp pangs of hunger gnawing at my insides. I poked my head outside and realised that the ubiquitous highland drizzle had returned, shrouding the summit of Hyddgen in a drab grey blanket of moisture. For once I thanked the Lord for the fine, thin rain which always found its way into and under everything. If it continued through the dawn and for an hour or two into the daylight hours, it would be a tremendous aid to us in our search for victory. It would allow us to walk straight into the Anglo-Flemish camp, remaining invisible until the last moment, and would confuse the moribund enemy, as they struggled to understand what was happening and how their compatriots, at any distance beyond a few yards, were coping.

As I got dressed, I was assailed for a moment by doubts and fears. Big man or not, I was subject to human frailty like everyone else, and an arrow or a cold blade through the heart would kill me as swiftly and as surely as it would any other human. In my mind I saw the lovely, gentle face of my beloved Mared. The warm smile was not there, only a veil of sadness with concern etched into those large, soulful eyes. Who was she so worried about? Dare I think her concern was for me? No, it was undoubtedly for Owain, her 'Golden One'. The best I could hope for was that it was mostly for Owain and, maybe, just a little for me... Would I live to see my love again? I shook myself and forced my doubts and fears into the background. There was no place in battle for the faint-hearted. A big lump like me should be more confident than most.

I stepped out of my tent, straightened my back and strode over to Owain's command tent, a battered helm in the crook of my left arm and my battleaxe gripped firmly in the other. The guard recognised me and grinned, murmuring a quiet '*Bore da*, Gruffudd,' as I bent under the flap to enter. Owain and a dozen of his commanders and senior officers greeted me briskly and Owain directed me to a makeshift chair in the half-circle facing him.

'You have not missed anything, Gruffudd. I was about to explain our strategy for today. Our plan is a very simple one and it is imperative, not only that the commanders ensure their own troops understand exactly what their particular mission is, but that they have a good grasp of the big picture and how every company will be contributing to the success of the plan. Now as you know, Beauchamp has had to surround the base of this mountain with troops to ensure that we do not escape down one of the more difficult slopes. He has realised, of course, that the only feasible side from which to launch an attack would be the western slopes and he has kept most of his army here in readiness. Nevertheless, I would estimate that at least a third of his forces have had to be deployed to cover the other three sides. This, of course, means that we will be outnumbered for a considerable period this morning by only two to one... and our strategy is based on defeating the force already here before the reinforcements arrive to support them. Now, having consulted with some among us who are native to this area, I am assured that while the Flemish camp is situated on good, hard ground, you only have to travel a short distance to the left or to the right and you are into very soggy marshland. A man in heavy armour would sink to his knees pretty quickly in such a bog and long, heavy swords and lances could be wielded only with difficulty in such conditions.'

I glanced quickly across and observed that Owain had chosen a short sword instead of his magnificent battle sword which he wielded with such power when astride his beloved Llwyd y Bacsie. I was glad that the noble warhorse was safely stabled with the other horses in the caves some miles away. Horses would be of no use in this battle.

'An essential feature of this strategy is the need for complete surprise. The enemy must not know that they are under attack until the killing starts, hence no initial longbow salvo – just a sudden, totally unexpected but murderous attack, the idea being to cut a swathe right through the centre of the hard ground, dividing the enemy in two. Then, a preordained half of our number, commanded by Tudur, will force those to the right side back and, hopefully into the marshes where they will be a lot easier to pick off. The other half of our army, under the command of Rhys Gethin, will force those on the left back and into the marshland on that side. At the forefront of the initial attack will be the fifty or so available axemen, who will bear the brunt of the struggle to cut the enemy force in two. They will be led by Rhys Ddu. I will be at the head of *Y Cedyrn*, the sixty members of my personal guard, and we will be poised to deal with any unexpected attack, or to support whichever of our companies is having problems in overcoming the enemy. So, a simple plan, but a plan which may not be so simple to achieve for all that. Be sure to impress upon your men that the first twenty minutes of this battle will be crucial and they must fight like demons from hell. Any questions?'

He stared at his three leading commanders: his brother Tudur, Rhys Gethin and Rhys Ddu. The three stared back at him, relaxed but confident. Evidently satisfied, Owain stood up and we all instantly followed suit.

'We are ready. Today we enter the jaws of death to achieve victory in the name of Owain Glyndŵr, by the Grace of God, Prince of Wales.' There was an almost manic light in Rhys Gethin's eyes as he roared his salute, repeated enthusiastically by everyone in the command tent. Then the time for words was over and they all trouped out in a tense silence, bristling with aggression as they went to seek their respective companies to ensure that the plan was clearly understood by all. Owain rose to his feet, moving with a feline grace; a patient tiger, his whole body like a great, wound-up spring, ready to release huge reserves of muscle power to overcome its prey.

'The day of reckoning is upon us, Gruffudd, let us pray that we both get through it victorious and unharmed. Victory will be a huge boost to us in so many ways, and I can send you back to care for the Lady Mared and the girls, for they must surely be missing you.'

'Maybe you will manage to find the time to see them also, if only for a few days, my lord. If they are missing me, how much more are they missing you?'

Owain closed his eyes and sighed. 'I am sure they are, my friend, I'm sure they are. There are times, though, when a ruler must choose his priorities and, unfortunately, affairs of state often mean that family considerations have to remain secondary.'

For a moment the golden eyes looked troubled but the expression was rapidly replaced by a confident smile.

'And now, axeman, be off with you to find Rhys Ddu, who is probably haranguing your colleagues on the importance of following his commands on pain of death. And Gruffudd... good luck!'

'Good luck to you, sire.' I hurriedly left him. I was too choked to say anything more.

Shortly before first light we began the slow, careful and stealthy journey down the western slopes of Hyddgen with the company of axemen in the vanguard. Rhys Ddu and I led the way, Rhys as commander and I as the axemen's representative on the Prince's command council. The drizzle was, if anything, heavier than it had been earlier but as we approached lower ground the heavy cloud cover began thinning out considerably. This only caused us to be more careful where we placed our feet, so as not to allow the loose scree to be accidentally kicked and career down the slopes, to alert the Anglo-Flemish forces.

Suddenly, we were at the bottom of the slope, hiding behind the last rock and heath cover. We were literally twenty yards from the first sentries and in the gloomy wet of a drizzly dawn we could see the dark shapes of tents and makeshift shelters, with the more imposing command tent slowly coming into focus towards the middle of the untidy settlement. Rhys Ddu summoned a dozen swordsmen who crouched low to advance stealthily towards the sentries. We crouched behind all available cover in a tense wait. If any of the sentries raised the alarm we would launch our attack immediately, but should our assassins manage their task in silence we would await their return. As luck would have it, the swordsmen accomplished their grim task in absolute silence. With all the sentries they could discover lying dead, throats cut, our presence had still not been detected.

Once the killers had returned to their unit, Rhys whispered orders which were quickly passed to the fifty axemen of the lead company. They were instructed to line up in five rows, each row ten abreast, and to maintain complete silence as they advanced carefully towards the nearest tents. They would wait until they were right outside the first tents before launching a full-scale, no-quarter, attack. The leading row of axemen was within ten yards of our goal when a Flemish soldier suddenly stepped out of a low shelter behind the first tent and started to relieve himself, yawning loudly. We all froze. The man finished and started to adjust his clothing. Then his jaw dropped as he saw what he must have thought were scores of outlandish, axe-wielding ghouls staring at him, silent but threatening. His mouth was opening to scream when a quick-thinker in the front rank raised his axe and threw it in one fluid movement. Before its victim could utter a sound, the blade struck him in the face, smashing through bone and gristle. A fountain of blood poured from his head before he collapsed, lifeless but twitching, on the ground. I stared at the axeman in horrified fascination, tinged with a detached admiration for his speed and skill. It was my old instructor,

Einion Fwyall, who, like his prince, was now well into his middle years.

'For God and Prince Owain,' roared the company of axemen, the battle cry taken up immediately by three hundred and fifty swordsmen following them swiftly as the ruthless Welsh attack was launched. The camp rapidly became a scene from hell as tents and bodies were torn to shreds by the swinging axes, the bloody dawn rent by the shouts and screams of more and more of the defenders as the Flemish army began to understand that they were, unbelievably, under intense attack.

Having achieved the planned total surprise and shock, the first twenty minutes of the battle went entirely our way. We rapidly forced our way through the centre of the enemy camp, the swinging axes of the lead company sweeping all before them, causing heavy casualties as they went. Then as the minutes passed we found ourselves coming up against alert, professional soldiers, well-armed and armoured, brought in from those parts of the camp where men had had sufficient time to get properly dressed and grab their weapons. Our progress slowed considerably but we were still moving forward at a steady pace. We, the axemen, were still leading the assault with each row of ten taking its turn as the front and most exposed row. We had rehearsed our method of achieving this through endless practice over many weeks, so that it became second nature to all of us. It was a simple idea which had to be executed perfectly on the battlefield. It involved each row doing the brunt of the head-to-head fighting for ten minutes and, at a shouted signal from an officer, the following four ranks of ten would double the space between each individual to allow the front rank to retreat between the lines of their comrades to become the fifth row and earn a much needed respite. The other four ranks would resume their original formations and the previous second rank would take over as the front rank, taking the strain for the next ten minutes.

My rank had just completed such a stint and had retreated to our fifth rank 'resting' position, just ahead of the first row of archers armed with short swords. I was one of three taking turns to guard our left flank from the attentions of enemy swordsmen when I stumbled into a pothole, falling forward onto my knees. I struggled to stand up as quickly as I could, conscious that my back was turned to the enemy. Suddenly a voice behind me shouted in strangely accented Welsh, warning me of danger behind me…

'Gruffudd, *y tu ôl iti!*'

In the act of rising I swung myself around, at the same time lifting my axe in the defensive position, double head sideways-on in front of my face, as I had been taught by Einion Fwyall many years before. An enemy sword blade struck the axehead with a resounding clang. Had I been half a second slower the sword would have split my face in two. All at once I was consumed with rage. I jabbed the sharp point at the front of the axe head into the enemy's chest. As the man staggered backwards I reversed my axe and swung it at his neck with all my strength. I felt the jarring of contact, though the man had skilfully swayed backward to take some of the force out of the blow. He dropped slowly to his knees, his head still partly attached to his body but at a grotesque angle. He began to keel over before his head slowly slithered sideways and parted company with his shoulders in a fountain of blood and rolled towards my feet. It came to a halt against my right boot, face up, eyes glazed. For a second I froze in horror. Oddly, the expression in the blue eyes conveyed neither pain, horror, nor fear, but rather a strangely muted surprise. Only then did I look for the man whose warning had saved my life. It was the Englishman, Tom Easton. We had now been separated in the ongoing mêlée but he was still shooting glances across to confirm that I had regained my feet. I raised my axe in gratitude and he grinned before having to concentrate hurriedly on defending himself once more.

I forced my aching arms to continue the relentless swinging of my bloodied axe, wondering why the enemy was not concentrating efforts on resisting our progress which would soon cut their army in two. The answer quickly became apparent. Having failed to halt our initial onslaught, some quick-thinking commander had decided that they would counterattack our forces on both sides simultaneously at a point where they might cut through to split our army in two, effectively surrounding the lead half while blocking the advance of the other half. They would certainly have the numbers to hold up the second part of our force while putting the front section under tremendous pressure. Fortunately, Owain and his elite guards had been holding back for just such a moment. He quickly realised the danger posed by the Anglo-Flemish ploy and led his men at the charge in amongst the attackers. Although only sixty in number, Glyndŵr's personal guards were all hard, experienced, highly-trained professionals who had seen service in many armies and to whom physical fitness was a matter of great personal pride. Their deployment was to be the defining moment of the battle. There was something almost superhuman about the way they tore into their opponents and their expertise at close-quarter fighting made an instant impression. The enemy rapidly discovered that this was a group of hand-picked killers, as their handiwork caused gaps to appear in the enemy ranks. The faces of the soldiers replacing the fallen dead began to show consternation as they realised how ineffective they were in standing up to these ferocious men. Gradually those expressions changed from disquiet to fear and shortly to panic. Some members of *Y Cedyrn* had captured the colours of the Flemings within minutes of joining the fray and after some fifteen minutes had forced home such a terrifying onslaught that, all of a sudden, their opponents started taking flight backwards in numbers. There is nothing like seeing your compatriots fleeing in panic on a battlefield to cause total loss of heart among even the most steadfast. Moreover, seeing your opponents running away provides the successful force with much additional stamina and courage. Soon, all of the enemy were fleeing the field and heading into the marshy ground on either side where many floundered, desperately trying to get out of their heavy armour and throwing away their swords in their eagerness to escape with their lives. Lines of reinforcements summoned from other areas around Hyddgen halted in amazement as they watched their compatriots fleeing the battle, and soon they too hurriedly headed south down the Hyddgen Valley, emulating their defeated colleagues. As if on cue, the clouds gradually cleared and the drizzle was steadily replaced by warm rays of June sunshine, greeting us into a brave new world.

Owain's first command as we all stared in disbelief at the Flemings running headlong down the valley was to call us to a halt.

'Hold there, men. There will be no pursuit for we do not have the stamina for it and, frankly, such a move would only show the enemy just how weak we are. Instead, let me salute you for fighting so magnificently in your half-starved state against a force more than twice our strength.

'In the end we won the day due to the tremendous effort of the axemen and the ruthless professionalism of *Y Cedyrn*. Having said that, the whole army, and some of you were fighting in the bloody horror of battle for the first time, displayed incredible courage and fortitude. I salute you, every one of you, for a victory which will send echoes around Wales during the next days and weeks, filling our countrymen with enthusiasm and pride. It will also send shivers of dread through the Marcher Lords as well as Bolingbroke and his nobles in London. As for the English citizens in the border towns of Chester, Shrewsbury, Hereford and Gloucester, I would wager they will soon be seeking opportunities to negotiate a truce with us by offering us much-needed gold and silver, in return for their safety.'

Owain's words were greeted with enthusiastic cheering as a huge feeling of relief and satisfaction swept through the men at having achieved what had seemed like an impossible feat of arms. Now they turned eagerly towards the supply wagons in search of food. Owain had anticipated the rush for food and had already stationed his personal guards around the food wagons to ensure an orderly system of distributing bread and other basics as a temporary measure, while the cooks searched for meat and the necessary ingredients to prepare an early evening feast for the victorious army. When Ednyfed ap Siôn reported our casualty figures to Owain later that afternoon, we were pleasantly surprised to learn that our total casualties were thirty-seven killed and two dozen injured, though none of the injuries were of a serious or disabling nature. I have to admit that I was saddened by the news that one member of *Y Cedyrn*, Edryd ap Hafgan, had been killed, for he was the guard who had welcomed me with a cheery smile into the command tent early that morning, an event which now seemed an age ago. It was difficult to believe that Edryd's easy camaraderie and smile were gone from this world for ever.

The following morning, squads of men took it in turns to move the bodies of the enemy dead to a natural hollow at the base of the mountain. We counted two hundred and thirty-four. Following post-battle custom, most of the victorious soldiers went among them, stripping the corpses of any usable clothing, weapons and adornments. Later we covered the bodies with rocks and boulders. Then we struck camp and made our way back to our original base at Esgair y Ffordd, taking the surviving Flemish tents and shelters with us, since our own camp had been destroyed. We were halfway to the erstwhile secret base, enjoying a fine sunny morning when we saw our civilian helpers, male and female, coming to meet us and singing our praises. We were heroes already in the highlands, for news of battle travels far and fast.

As the army approached the cheering group, the majority of the women began running towards us, laughing and searching through the faces in the ranks. Many gave delighted gasps of joy at seeing a loved one and, defying protocol, ran straight to their favourite to embrace him with relief and happiness. Few noticed, as I did, the minority who ran alongside all the ranks without seeing the face they were searching for, nor how the tears of joy suddenly became tears of grief and despair, with many falling to the ground, beating their fists on the rock-strewn earth, overwhelmed by the cruel reality of their loss. Such is the effect of battle on both sides, for while the horrors of maiming and killing are borne by the combatants, the desolation of death and the gnawing pangs of grief and loss are also the lot of many innocents, especially women and children.

14

O UR VICTORY AT the Battle of Hyddgen signalled a huge change in our fortunes. Owain quickly became revered as the latest in a long line of heroic Welsh war leaders, his mantle as the long awaited Son of Prophecy assured. A trickle of local chieftains soon became a flood as scores of *uchelwyr* and others of the lesser squirearchy who, until now, had been loath to show their hand were, as a result of Hyddgen, won over wholeheartedly to our cause. Many wanted to join Owain's forces immediately, itching for action, whilst others brought the promise of direct action in localised insurrection all over Wales. Hundreds of individuals, many of them seasoned soldiers having served in English armies in Scotland, Ireland and France, came to swear allegiance to their Prince. As reports of Welsh success at Hyddgen spread into England, many exiles working as farm labourers, and Welsh students at Oxford and Cambridge, forsook their labours and hurried back to their homeland to join what had now become a truly national struggle.

Coping with this great flood of support, with its attendant organisational problems, was a major challenge which Owain embraced with enthusiasm and vigour. His enthusiasm was infectious and all his senior officers, including some very capable individuals from among the new arrivals, were quick to offer strong support. 'Glyndŵr's Children' as they were to become known, now numbered almost three thousand men. Half their number were soldiers with varying degrees of battle experience, while the others were little more than enthusiastic amateurs. Owain and his officers were acutely aware that his army was far from ready to meet professional English troops in large-scale, pitched battles. Much more experience and training was required before the Welsh could change their traditional tactics of lightning strikes, surprise attacks and proven guerrilla action against an enemy so numerically superior, boasting professionally trained and equipped forces.

With the Tudur brothers, Rhys and Gwilym, continuing to cause mayhem in the north, attacking and stealing the English King's tax wagons from the tax collectors and their inadequate military escorts, and disrupting commerce between the small English boroughs settled around the strong ring of coastal castles, Owain was reinforcing Bolingbroke's concerns that the Glyndŵr revolt was rapidly developing into a full-scale national rebellion. This could soon become a serious threat to English control in Wales and even to Henry's position as King of England. Relations with the French, the Irish and the restless Scots were already worsening by the day. He could ill afford a major military confrontation in Wales in terms of manpower or cost.

One morning, a few weeks after the battle of Hyddgen, I was invited to an early breakfast with Owain in his tent. Despite his punishing schedule in the aftermath of our recent success, he was looking rested and relaxed when I entered his imposing tent, inherited from Sir William Beauchamp after the justiciar's hasty departure from the area.

'I hope you have slept well, Gruffudd, for I would like you to be at your sharpest this morning,' he enthused as I greeted him.

I took my seat, glancing up at him in surprise. 'If I had

known I would be required to pay for my breakfast with an instant poem, sire, I would have brought my quills along.'

He smiled indulgently at my mild effrontery. 'No, Master Poet, it is not your poetry I require but the chance to probe that astute brain of yours. And I'll throw in a free breakfast to please you.'

I grinned appreciatively and we sat facing each other across the table in the amiable and relaxed manner of two friends, secure in the bonds of trust and mutual respect, nurtured and honed over many years.

We were interrupted by the sentry coming in to announce the arrival of breakfast, and two young female servants followed him in, laden with plates on wooden trays. One bore the hallmarks of a young girl newly transformed into womanhood, and who was very aware of that fact. Her dark hair was long and carefully combed and her equally dark eyes were lustrous and sparkling with promise, while a faint yet tantalising smile hovered around her generous lips. The other, though only a few years younger, was pretty but still cocooned in the innocence of a child. They nervously placed everything on the table, including clean knives, spoons and pewter tankards. I have to confess I was not altogether unmoved by the elder girl's attractiveness, particularly her own awareness of it and its potential power over men.

Owain thanked them and the budding temptress curtsied and asked, 'Will there be anything else, sire? Oh… and cook sends you her respects, Your Highness.' She blushed prettily as she realised how close she had come to forgetting to pass on the cook's regards.

'No, everything is as Gruffudd and I would wish it, my dear. You are Awen, are you not? Dafydd ap Ithel, the longbow champion's daughter.'

Awen lowered her eyes and looked even more embarrassed. 'Yes, sire. And this is my younger sister, Dyddgu.' Now it was the younger girl's turn to blush.

'Well, I thank you both. Be sure to present my regards to cook... and to your father, of course.'

The two quickly left and we could hear them giggling as they scampered back to the kitchens.

'Awen,' I murmured dreamily. 'What a lovely name. A muse, an inspiration.'

'Oh ho, Master Bard! This particular Awen has obviously touched a nerve in your romantic soul,' Owain chortled. 'Are we to see this moving moment transformed into another inspired *cywydd*, I wonder?'

'Not at all,' I demurred. 'I am more familiar with the war axe than the pen these days...'

'I hardly think the axe was in your mind when that young lady caused your eyes to glaze over... and do not deny it because I saw your reaction when she entered the tent...' Owain laughed again, delighted that he had caught me out.

There were no further words between us for a while as we tucked into tasty, newly-baked bread and thick, delicious slices of cold roast pork, washed down with small beer. After we had both eaten our fill he pushed the plate away, sipped the last of the small beer and swiftly assumed a more business-like demeanour.

'I have done a great deal of thinking while organising our new set-up, Gruffudd.'

He paused and slowly scratched his forked beard, the golden eyes staring contemplatively at me. His mind seemed fixed on I know not what, though it must have been important. Then, with a characteristic shrug of the shoulders, Owain was very much back in the present and eager to start.

'Let's sum up our current situation, as I see it. I shall then want to know firstly, whether you agree with my summation and, secondly, how you believe we can gain as much advantage as possible while the English are wrong-footed.'

'I shall do so with pleasure. However, I doubt whether any ideas I may suggest will improve on the plans which you have, I'm sure, already made and thought through, my lord. You are far more experienced in politics and in military matters than I will ever be.'

'As ever, you enjoy putting yourself down, Gruffudd Fychan. Look, I need fresh thoughts… I need your opinions, not because of any damn experience you may or may not have, but because I believe you have an incisive mind and I know, through listening to your poetry, and from conversing with you over the years, that you have the knack of wading through all side issues and recognising the crux of the matter, whatever the subject may be. You see, as *Tywysog*, I may be too close to everything to do that. You obviously cannot be totally objective in assessing our fortunes, either intellectually or emotionally, but you do possess the wonderful ability to detach yourself from a problem in order to examine it logically and carefully. That is what I need from you.'

He paused for breath before continuing in a quieter tone, 'All you need do is think in your usual style and tell me, honestly, whether you agree or not with my thoughts on the whole situation. Then I would like you to state, in broad terms, how you think we can successfully rub English noses in the muck and take control of the whole of Wales.'

'Very well,' I responded, trying to sound light and confident, though I still felt that he was expecting too much from my intellect, such as it is.

'It is accepted,' Owain began, 'that in rebelling against English rule we are, at best, taking on a very difficult and dangerous task. It is a task which even our most successful warrior princes have, ultimately, failed to achieve. There are many in Wales today who believe it to be an impossible task for any contemporary Welsh leader. It is easy to understand their misgivings. The English are a far bigger nation… many times our number. They are much wealthier and, having been at war with us, the Irish, the Scots and the French variously over many years, they can raise large, professional armies packed with experienced soldiers very quickly. They have managed to dominate us for almost two hundred years, largely due to a chain of formidable stone-built castles, most of which can be provisioned and reinforced from the sea. We do not have a tradition of warfare at sea, and we have no vessels that can match theirs, let alone the experience and skills for combat at sea.

'The question is, do we have any advantages which could work in our favour? And I believe that, at present, we do. Firstly, the usurper King Henry IV is probably at his weakest. There are many within the English nobility who do not believe he has a rightful claim to his throne. He has to be on his guard against these people all the time, and needs the full support of Parliament to get his policies through. Many of the common people believe that King Richard is still alive and would support any credible challenge to Henry. He is also surrounded by hostile nations – the Scots, the Irish, the French, and now us. We also know that financially he is very insecure, and has difficulty in financing an army of any size for more than a few weeks. There are some other advantages too. For instance, although our forces are much fewer in number and, by and large, less experienced and trained, we are blessed with mountains and hills and wooded valleys not suited for what the English would regard as conventional warfare. Our traditional hit-and-run style of attack is ideal for such conditions. Then there is the weather. We tend to get far more rain than England. Our mountain streams pour flood water down into the valleys on occasion, which can bog down a large army in heavy armour and create real opportunities for us to give them a very bad time. Again, very importantly, all our men are volunteers who believe in the cause for which they fight. The English soldiers are pressed men who are forcibly conscripted into service for reasons which may not be very clear to them, at least some of the time.'

Owain paused for breath, staring at me intently before taking up the theme.

'And now, my friend, we have, since Hyddgen, a new and potent advantage. For the first time since we started this struggle last year, we have a groundswell of goodwill and pride which has filled the hearts of *uchelwyr* and ordinary folk alike. I would say that we now have the wholehearted support of the majority of our people. At last, they have come to believe that we have a fighting chance of achieving full independence for our country. Think of all the wonderful changes it will bring to the lives of every Welsh person – a return to the laws of Hywel Dda; the reinstatement of Welsh as the language of commerce, of the law courts, of society generally; and the freedom to conduct business on an equal footing with everyone.

It would also mean the introduction of a fairer taxation system, so that no one would face unreasonable or crippling taxes.'

Again he paused, his face totally animated by the vision of what independence would mean. 'Well, what say you, Gruffudd?'

'My lord, you paint a pleasing picture of an independent Wales, but I am not convinced that it could be achieved by our traditional hit-and-run tactics. You will, eventually, require large, well-drilled forces to take on Bolingbroke. Unless you can beat him in set-piece battles, our success will be nothing more than fleeting and temporary.'

'That is absolutely correct,' Owain conceded. 'Moreover, we will need to reach that level of success within the next few years because, as time passes, so will Henry's hold on the throne of England be strengthened.'

'I'm sorry, Owain, but I still feel that there are many other matters which must be considered before our country can be a complete state, so that Welshmen can hold their heads high in the knowledge that they are citizens of a civilised country with a *Tywysog* who is wise and cultured, as well as an accomplished warrior.'

I stole a glance at him, wondering whether he might have been irritated by my presumption. I was surprised to see a broad grin on his face.

'Well, go on. Enlighten me.' He leaned back in his chair, his eyes alive with anticipation.

'I look at the world around me,' I responded. 'I look at other countries and I see that those with a strong, successful society have a number of things in common. The rule of law is one basic necessity. Another is an enlightened ruler who is concerned about the welfare of his people. Knowledge is another powerful ingredient. Knowledge goes hand-in-hand with culture and science and power. Knowledge must be nurtured through a system of education, providing learning opportunities for everyone from the young right through to adults. Another essential is religion. Every successful ruler has strong and favourable ties with senior church leaders. The church has a very strong hold over the mass of a country's population. A wise ruler is always in a strong position if he has the support of the Church. Animosity between ruler and the Church weakens both, and must be avoided at all costs. Finally, every successful country needs a strong economy to improve the lot of its people and to strengthen the country's influence in its dealings with other countries.'

I stopped as Owain jumped to his feet and started clapping his hands.

'I knew it, I knew it!' he shouted excitedly. 'I knew you would confirm my thinking... but I had to hear you say so.'

For a moment I stared at him in astonishment, bewildered by his almost childlike enthusiasm. He strode over to me and clapped my back hard.

'Gruffudd, I can always trust you to turn up trumps. I'm sure you will be pleased to hear that I am already working on some of your "cornerstones", and I have firm plans for the others to be put in motion when the time is right. I have already sent a letter to the Scottish King, Robert III, suggesting ways in which we could support each other in making war on Henry. I shall be writing shortly to the Irish leaders and to King Charles VI of France along the same lines. I am in contact with some of the most powerful leaders of the Church in Wales as well. I have had no firm commitments as yet, but I suspect that following our recent

Hyddgen success, the position will soon change. I have given a great deal of thought to a new system of education, including the setting up of two Welsh universities, one in the north and the other in the south. So you see, old friend, we both seem to be of like mind on the essentials for setting up a state we can be proud of.'

Owain stood up and wandered over to the window, staring out in silence for a moment. 'I have one more matter I would like you to give me your views upon.'

He turned back to me once again, stroking his beard thoughtfully. 'Now that our struggle has become a truly national one, how can we convince Bolingbroke that the great majority of Welshmen are now giving me their full support? How can we make the situation as worrying as possible for him? What I am really asking, I suppose, is how can we make the most effective use of our new, much enlarged military forces?'

I thought for a moment. 'Well, if I were King of England, I would love to meet Owain Glyndŵr in a set battle. Yes, he would have a sizeable army but I would probably have an even bigger one, made up of experienced warriors. My adversary would have some seasoned troops but also a large number of untried, and not too well-trained novices. What would I dislike most? Without question I would hate having to deal with a dozen or more smaller war bands playing havoc all over Wales, scaring the life out of the English settlers in the boroughs around my castles, disrupting trade and the free movement of my law officers and administrators, and even laying siege to some of the castles. Such action could be organised in every part of the country, virtually all the time. I would be powerless to prevent it, for I would have neither the manpower nor the money to finance punitive expeditions all over the place. Is that similar to your own thoughts on best tactics?'

'It is precisely the same,' Owain laughed delightedly. 'I shall now speak with all my commanders and get them to go back to their respective areas with instructions to upset English rule in any way they can. They must also ensure that the raw volunteers in their war bands learn strict discipline in action, to back up the weapons training we have introduced already.'

He turned and beckoned me to follow him outside. 'Now, I have news which I think you will welcome.' There was a mischievous glint in his eye. 'Which way is due north from this spot?'

I began to raise my arm to point, then dropped it to my side as I realised what he was telling me. 'Are you saying we are going home?' I tried hard to keep the excitement and disbelief out of my voice.

'That rather depends on whether you regard Dolbadarn, our fortress in the fastnesses of Snowdonia, as home.'

'It is not the destination I would have expected. Actually, I imagined I would be returning to my regular role as your lady's protector,' I answered stiffly.

Owain assumed the annoying grin which he reserves for teasing me on occasion. After a long pause he said in a placatory tone. 'It's alright, you can stop frowning. Mared should have arrived at Dolbadarn last night. I decided it was time to move her and her ladies away from Anglesey. My spies in the March tell me that Henry is scraping together another expedition to lay waste to north Wales and curb our cousins who have been busy for weeks creating the kind of havoc we are planning for the remainder of the country in the coming weeks.'

Dolbadarn, perched high above the lake known as Llyn Padarn, had been used by Llywelyn the Great to guard the strategically important Llanberis Pass. I had visited it the previous year when Owain and a small group of personal guards had spent a winter of hardship in the small, semi-derelict, stone-built castle. The thought of housing my lady in such an inhospitable place shocked me to the core. Owain must have read my thoughts for he cut in quickly.

'Don't be angry, Gruffudd. What you do not know is that, ever since leaving Dolbadarn in early spring, I have had local masons and carpenters there every day refurbishing the curtain walls and the timber roofs of the various buildings. This winter there will be additional fireplaces in the hall and most of the sleeping quarters. The kitchens too have been made weatherproof. My only regret is that it is so small. Even now it will only accommodate a very small court, a few servants and a garrison of up to thirty men. But fear not, Mared and the girls will be cosy enough. It will also be provisioned with sufficient food, firewood and arms to last the whole winter if need be. In any case, it will be too cold for anyone to lay siege to Dolbadarn in winter. Any force foolish enough to attempt it would be frozen to death.'

I smiled sheepishly. 'You have thought of everything, sire. I'm sorry for my lack of faith.'

'Your concern for the Lady Mared does you credit, Master Bard. But it seems to have blinded you for a moment... on this occasion,' he added, giving me a strange look.

I felt myself blushing furiously and tried to apologise further but he simply raised his hand palm forward to stop me, the odd look quickly replaced by an indulgent smile.

'No apologies necessary,' my friend. 'As I said, your concern does you credit and I thank you for it.'

'Will you be joining me on the journey?' I asked, to change the subject.

'No. I would like you to set off tomorrow morning. I will give you an escort of twenty archers and six pikemen. You will all be mounted, so you should reach Dolbadarn in three days, God willing. There are twenty or so armed men there who have been the fort's garrison for more than two months. They are all men of Snowdonia. I want you to send them home to their families for a week before reporting for duty to Rhys ap Tudur in the Bangor area. The locals will inform them of Rhys's whereabouts. You and your escort will form the new garrison. I will stay on here for a week or so. I need to appoint local commanders for the various areas within the March and the so-called "sovereign lands". Some of them will be new to our cause and will need to be informed in detail of our current strategy, and our tactics for carrying out that strategy. A system of communication needs to be set up between the area commanders and me, and also between commanders of neighbouring areas, to organise quick reinforcement and other assistance if, and when, needed. I reckon I will be ready to bring along the northern elements, comprising some two thousand men, in ten days' time. That force will be divided in two during the journey. Rhys Gethin will take charge of the Powys men and head for the Corwen area, while I bring the Gwynedd men back to the north west.'

'Why Corwen?'

'Rhys Gethin will need to find a suitably secluded area to make camp and to send spies to Ruthin and neighbouring English boroughs. We need to find out how our "friend", Lord de Grey de Ruthin, is behaving these days. He is responsible in large part for our current situation and it is about time he discovered that I, too, am capable of causing much suffering. I have plans in which he will play a significant, albeit an unwilling part!'

I saw the cold, implacable look in the tawny eyes and despite the warmth of the summer sun, I shivered and almost felt sorry for Reginald de Grey.

Also by the author:

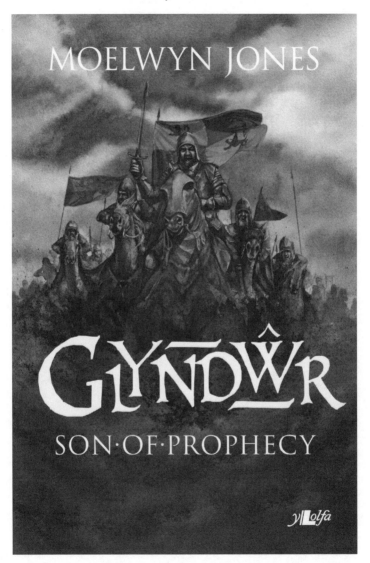

MOELWYN JONES

GLYNDŴR

SON·OF·PROPHECY

yLolfa

£6.99

Glyndŵr: To Arms! is just one of a whole range of publications from Y Lolfa. For a full list of books currently in print, send now for your free copy of our new full-colour catalogue. Or simply surf into our website

www.ylolfa.com

for secure on-line ordering.

TALYBONT CEREDIGION CYMRU SY24 5HE
e-mail ylolfa@ylolfa.com
website www.ylolfa.com
phone (01970) 832 304
fax 832 782

Ask for a print quote!
01970 832 304